Fortune-Teller

When I was younger, I used to be afraid of the mechanical gypsy fortune-teller, with her faded red taffeta skirts and the ugly wart on her chin. I had thought she was a real person trapped for eternity in her glass booth, so old she could only move in painful-looking jerks. Now Madame Zaza yanked to life, passing her mechanical hands over the lit crystal ball, her rubber face twisting into an expression that was supposed to represent mystical concentration. A little white card emerged from a larger slot below the penny slot.

"Read it," Gretchen said, jabbing me with her elbow. Whenever there was a boy within fifty miles, Gretchen's elbow took on a life of its own, poking and prodding me, as if it had been taking jerking lessons from Madame Zaza.

"It says, A ROOM WITHOUT MIRRORS IS LIKE A BODY WITHOUT A SOUL."

"What's *that* supposed to mean?" she asked.

**Other Apple paperbacks
you will enjoy:**

Truth or Dare
  by Susan Beth Pfeffer

Starting with Melodie
  by Susan Beth Pfeffer

Adorable Sunday
  by Marlene Fanta Shyer

A Season of Secrets
  by Alison Cragin Herzig
  and Jane Lawrence Mali

Starstruck
  by Marisa Gioffre

The Trouble with Soap
  by Margery Cuyler

Baby-Snatcher
  by Susan Terris

A, My Name is Ami
  by Norma Fox Mazer

THIRTEEN

Candice F. Ransom

AN
APPLE
PAPERBACK

SCHOLASTIC INC.
New York Toronto London Auckland Sydney

For my mother,
who had to put up with me

ISBN 0-590-40192-0

Lyrics from "Mr. Tambourine Man," by Bob Dylan used by permission. © 1964 Warner Bros. Inc. All rights reserved.

12 11 10 9 8 7 6 5 4 3 2   6 7 8 9/8 0 1/9

Chapter 1

Exactly three weeks and two and a half days after my thirteenth birthday, I finally turned thirteen. Talk about a delayed reaction!

I was standing in the second-floor kitchen of the rambling old beach house my parents rented for a week each August, sandy linoleum gritting beneath my bare feet. My best friend in the whole world was sitting on the floor, her strawberry-blond hair wisping out around her face, painting her toenails a particularly repulsive shade of salmon pink. Gretchen's parents rented the first floor of the house every summer, but Gretch and I were so inseparable, we spent nights together as well as the long, sun-drenched days. One night she'd stay with me in my cramped, stuffy bedroom; the next I'd share her couch-that-made-into-a-bed on the sleeping porch down-stairs.

The sunburn I'd acquired that day was starting to prickle, but I was glad. Even if I looked like I'd been dipped in Mercuro-chrome, it was better than being fish-belly white. Any color at all made my legs seem less skinny. I was wearing cutoffs and a lemon yellow cropped top trimmed with eyelet ruffles from my nonexistent bust to the hem. The ruffles helped fill me out. But my cut-offs, newly washed and skin tight as dictated by some unwritten law, pointed up the dismal truth: I had no hips, no waist, no stomach, no rear, no nothing but high hopes that *someday* I'd be curvy like Gretch. Even my dull brown hair was straight.

On the windowsill, Gretchen's transistor was blasting out tinny music, as usual. Our house was only a block from the ocean and our windows faced out onto the street. I could see people streaming down the side-walk in front of our place, returning from the beach with the plodding, shuffling step and the neon glow of the all-day sun-worshipper. Some of them were on the verge of all-night misery, only they didn't know it yet, and others could barely drag their beach towels.

I said to Gretch, who was stuffing wads

of toilet paper between the toes on her left foot, "Aren't you finished yet? Who looks at your feet anyhow?"

"Maybe *you* should pay more attention to your own feet, Kobie Roberts," she shot back.

If I thought I could improve my appearance by painting my toenails, I would have owned a nail polish company by now. But I was more interested in sneaking up to the tenant's room on the third floor.

"If you don't hurry," I warned her, "he'll be back and then we'll never get a chance to go through his things."

"I don't want to snoop in that man's room. What's the point? All we'll find are some stinky old socks and a picture of his mother or something."

I snorted. "A picture of his mother! You've got to be kidding! We might find pictures all right, but they won't be of his mother. They'll be his girl friends."

There were only two cubbyhole rooms upstairs, the sloping walls covered with a busy turquoise and purple wallpaper that made you want to run around on all fours, snapping at people's ankles. Because the third-floor garret had no kitchen, it was usually rented to a single man. Last year's tenant slept until noon, then went out and didn't come home until the sun was coming up. But this year's tenant hung around his rooms with aggravating regularity, making it impossible for us to sneak up there.

"He could be back any minute," I urged. "He only goes to the corner for a paper and some milk."

"Imagine a grown man drinking milk," Gretchen said scornfully. "How interesting can his room be if he drinks milk without being made to?"

She had a point. But we had *always* spied on the third-floor tenants, ever since our parents started coming to Ocean City five years ago. It was *tradition*.

"Besides," she went on, "it's so *juvenile*, Kobie. Rummaging through a guy's bureau drawers. Kids' stuff."

Juvenile was a word Gretchen managed to insert in every other sentence this summer. Directed at me, naturally. Although we were both the same age — our birthdays only six weeks apart — Gretch seemed to be skipping ahead of me, and not just in the figure department, either.

We used to agree on absolutely everything, but lately Gretchen was sort of touchy. She didn't want to do much except work on her tan, paint her toenails, and listen to the radio. Some things we'd agree on forever, like that Johnny Sea, a boy from school, was a creep of the first magnitude, but one thing that had bugged me all week was her stupid radio. When I asked her to turn it off, or even down a little, she insisted her favorite song was on, she couldn't. Every song seemed to be her favorite song, and they were all sung by people with dumb names like Sonny and Cher or the Animals.

Now I opened my mouth to fire back a smart reply to her "kids' stuff" remark, when the d.j. on the radio finally stopped begging everyone in Ocean City to come on down to Bull's for all the ribs it was humanly possible to eat in one sitting, and a new record came on.

A jangly electric guitar, underscored by purring bass, reached out and grabbed me. Then this singer with the slightest hint of a sob in his voice began singing:

"He-ey, Mr. Tambourine Man, play a
    song for me.
I'm not sleepy and there ain't no place
    I'm goin' to.
He-ey, Mr. Tambourine Man, play a
    song for me.
In the jingle-jangle mornin' I'll come
    followin' you."

My life changed.

I couldn't move. I stood there in the kitchen, stock-still, while the song poured over and around and through me until I was not only *in* the song, I *was* the song.

I had never felt that way before about anything, much less a record on the radio. A small part of me seemed to break away inside and drift upward, carried by the haunting lyrics. When the song ended, I knew I wasn't the same person I had been two minutes before. Vaguely, I remembered something about sneaking upstairs to the third floor, but for some reason I didn't want to go anymore.

"Hey, Gretch," I asked, thinking that even my own voice sounded different. "What was that song?"

Gretchen knew the Top 40 backward and forward. " 'Mr. Tambourine Man,' by the Byrds. Neat, isn't it?"

"When will it come on again? If we switch the station, do you think we could find somebody else playing it?"

She looked at me strangely. "What's *with* you? All week you've complained about my radio."

"Never mind. Are you done with your stupid toenails? Let's hit the boardwalk."

"I thought you wanted to go upstairs." She replaced the cap on the nail polish.

"Not anymore." I couldn't shake the weird feeling the song brought on. Before "Mr. Tambourine Man," I used to feel sort of starched inside, like I knew exactly what I wanted to do, even if my parents wouldn't always let me do it. Now my stomach felt like Jell-O and I wasn't sure about anything.

And then it hit me. I had finally, suddenly — and no doubt irreversibly — turned thirteen.

Had it been like this for Gretchen? Or had she stepped into thirteen on her birthday in June as easily as changing into a new pair of shoes? I wanted to ask her, but this new Jell-O-y me was too uncertain to put such crazy thoughts into words.

"Hurry up," I snapped instead. "I'm hungry."

She slipped into her flip-flops, admiring her pedicure. "What's with you all of a sudden?"

"Nothing." Not quite true, but I didn't think she'd believe me if I told her a song on the radio had transformed me from a kid into a teenager, even if she was my best friend.

Whatever had happened just then, I was stuck with it.

During the seven marvelous days of our vacation, Gretchen and I were allowed to run loose in Ocean City. Maybe it was the salt air, but at the beach our parents were definitely more lenient. Or maybe it was because we were in Maryland and the old rules didn't cross the state line with us. When we got back home to Virginia tomorrow, I knew from experience I'd have the rope around my neck again. But since this was our last night of vacation, I planned to enjoy my freedom to the hilt.

Tonight our folks were going to the Crab House. As Gretch and I both hated crabs, we were given a few dollars to "eat on the boardwalk" and if we had anything left over, we could blow it on rides or games at the amusement end of the boardwalk.

"Have something besides french fries," my mother had cautioned earlier, as she handed me two dollars. "Something nutritious, you hear me, Kobie?"

I fully intended to have something besides french fries, although cotton candy and caramel popcorn hardly fell into the category of nutritious foods.

Gretch and I raced each other to the sandy wooden steps a short block away. I looked past the stragglers coming in off the beach to the ocean. The tide was out and waves rolled in to the shore. It was a little early for the nighttime crowd — most people were taking showers, getting ready to go out to dinner. But there was an excitement just beginning to stir on the boardwalk, and the people looked more lively, unlike the sun-glazed drudges who scuffed up and down during the day, going to the public bathrooms or one of the stands for a drink.

"Eff-effs?" Gretchen asked me.

"Natch." I gave her a little shove and we threaded our way up the boardwalk, darting around potbellied men with sun-burned knees and ridiculous straw hats.

The best french fries in Ocean City were made at Snicks 'N Snacks — shoelace potatoes double deep-fried with the skins on. I hung impatiently over the greasy wooden counter while a bored lady scooped up our orders. Gretch poured half a bottle of catsup into her paper cup, but I gobbled mine plain.

We walked slowly toward the amusement end of the boardwalk, cramming fries in until we were both so thirsty it was like we'd been lost in the Sahara for a month.

"We'll get a Coke at the very next stand," I said.

"Let's split one," Gretch suggested. "That way we'll have more money to spend."

We shared a Coke, but we each bought our own ice cream sundaes, since Gretchen craved butterscotch and I couldn't live without hot fudge. The sundaes were so sweet, we split a hot dog "to cut the sugar," as Gretchen said, and then we had to have caramel popcorn at Dolly's to get the mustard taste out of our mouths.

By the time we reached the penny arcade, my stomach was already sending up signal flares, but I burped behind my hand and tried to ignore it. What was the point of eating junk if you didn't get a little sick? And anyhow, this was a better kind of sick than the way I felt whenever I ate brussels sprouts. A few games of skeet-ball and I'd be ready to hit the rides and still keep my supper down.

Gretchen had other ideas. "Let's have our fortunes told," she suggested. I could tell by the gleam in her blue eyes there must be a boy in the vicinity.

I craned my head to see past the pinball machines. Sure enough, on the far side of the room, a boy about fifteen or sixteen loitered next to Madame Zaza, the mechanical gypsy fortune-teller. "Do we have to?" I started to say, but then that thirteen - Mr. - Tambourine - Man - feeling swept over me again. I looked at the boy once more. He was cute, with blond hair that tumbled into his eyes and a T-shirt with the sleeves rolled up.

I had never approached a boy before, afraid he'd run away screaming. The closest I'd come to flirting with a guy was at

10

a party I went to last year. It was the dumbest affair of the century. The girls had barricaded themselves on one side of the room, talking too loud over the records, while the boys had camped out near the refreshments, punching each other and standing in a tight knot like a wagon train circled against an attack.

Toward the end of the evening, I had worked up enough nerve to ask a red-haired kid named Hal if he'd hand me the potato chip bowl, which had a few broken chips in the bottom the guys had somehow overlooked. He had smiled as he passed it to me and I'd foolishly imagined maybe I had a chance. I had eaten a chip and smiled back. Then he'd said, "You eat potato chips funnier than anybody I ever saw," and left, dashing all my romantic hopes.

But things would be different tonight, I was certain. I was still in the spell of the song I had heard on the radio — anything was possible.

"What do we do?" I asked Gretchen.

"We'll both go up and have our fortunes told. Then I'll ask you for the time but you say you don't have a watch. Then I'll ask that guy if *he* has the time."

"What if he doesn't have a watch, either?"

Gretch shook her head and her strawberry-blond ponytail swished over her shoulders. "It won't matter. I'll ask him what street he lives on. That's what everybody does when they first meet somebody here. Maybe he's staying near us."

Doubts and the scarring memory of Hal pointing out my bad table manners made me hesitate. "What if it doesn't work?"

Gretchen was cool. "What's not to work? All we're really going to do is ask him the time. The rest follows."

"Unless he runs away," I muttered, but gamely tagged after my friend.

The blond boy was still there when we reached Madame Zaza, leaning negligently against the glass booth. He appraised us from under sheep-dog bangs.

Gretchen giggled, suddenly losing her cool, and asked me for a penny. "Hurry *up*," she insisted, as if Madame Zaza was going to vanish in a puff of smoke if we didn't feed our pennies into the slot that instant.

I fumbled for change in the pocket of my tight cut-offs, sweat popping out on my forehead as I realized two things: one, I was actually approaching a boy for the first time (not counting that feeble attempt over the empty potato chip bowl), and two, my stomach really and truly did *not* have room for french fries, a fudge sundae, caramel popcorn, Coke, half a hot dog with the works, "Mr. Tambourine Man," and the newness of being thirteen.

I fished out two pennies, swayed a little, and told Gretch, "I'll go first." I dropped my penny into the slot, praying Madame Zaza would send me an Alka-Seltzer tablet instead of a little white card with my fortune.

When I was younger, I used to be afraid of the mechanical gypsy fortune-teller, with her faded red taffeta skirts and the ugly wart on her chin. I had thought she was a real person trapped for eternity in her glass booth, so old she could only move in painful-looking jerks. Now Madame Zaza yanked to life, passing her mechanical hands over the lit crystal ball, her rubber face twisting into an expression that was supposed to represent mystical concentration. A little white card emerged from a larger slot below the penny slot. I snatched it like a drowning man clutching a lifesaver, hoping it would instruct me to go home and lie down immediately.

"Read it," Gretchen said, jabbing me with her elbow. Whenever there was a boy within fifty miles, Gretchen's elbow took on a life of its own, poking and prodding me, as if it had been taking jerking lessons from Madame Zaza.

"It says, A ROOM WITHOUT MIRRORS IS LIKE A BODY WITHOUT A SOUL."

"What's *that* supposed to mean?" she asked.

I shrugged. "How should I know? These fortunes are always dumb sayings, like 'He who travels alone, travels fastest.'" I wished I *were* traveling alone, heading for the restrooms. I looked at the card again. "It does sound odd. I think it should be a room without *windows*, not mirrors."

"My turn. Give me my penny."

I handed her a penny and tried to think stomach-settling thoughts while Madame Zaza did her thing over the crystal ball.

Gretchen read her fortune and then a strange look came over her face. She threw the card down on the sawdust-littered floor.

"What's it say?" I asked.

"Nothing. Just something stupid."

"It couldn't be any stupider than mine." I bent down, silently warning my stomach that I was *not* leaning over a toilet bowl, and picked up her card. Wiping off a sticky blob of cotton candy, I read the printed message: THERE ARE DARK DAYS AHEAD; DO NOT BE DISCOURAGED.

"Boy," I said weakly. "That *is* dumb. How could anybody not be discouraged knowing they've got dark days ahead? Just thinking about it would get me discouraged — "

"I told you it was nothing," Gretch said, her elbow stabbing me in the ribs again. Between my stomach and her elbow, I felt one of those dark days had been reserved for me, and it was here right now.

In a sweeter tone, Gretchen said, "Kobie, do you have the time?"

Remembering her plan, I looked at both my wrists as if I'd never before noticed they'd been attached to the ends of my arms for thirteen years and replied, "Sorry, I'm not wearing my watch." Or my thinking cap. Here we were getting ready to make a play for this boy and I was only two seconds away from upchucking over half the boardwalk.

But Gretchen was already asking Blondie for the time. He gave a little mocking laugh.

"Don't matter none to me what time it is. Day, night, it's all the same," he said, and right away I was impressed with his keen intelligence.

Faltering only a little, Gretch went on to Plan B. "What street are you staying on?"

"Twenty-third."

"I don't know that one," she said. "We're staying on Second and Baltimore."

"Oh, yeah. The big white house on the corner." He looked at Gretchen with interest, which was not surprising since she had a fantastic figure. I stood to one side, feeling greener by the minute. "What're you girls up to?"

Gretch's elbow flew out of control again and I knew she wanted me to answer this one, but I knew if I opened my mouth, they'd both be sorry.

Blondie gestured at me. "What's with her? Cat got her tongue?"

Gretchen screeched like a seagull, as if this was the funniest thing she'd ever heard. "She's just shy, that's all. When you get to know Kobie, she's really great." If Blondie knew what was good for him, he would *not* try to get acquainted with me. "We usually go on the rides," she went on. "Want to go with us?"

The rides! The very notion of spinning around on the Tilt-a-Whirl made my stomach roil. I tugged her sleeve. "Listen, Gretch — "

"That stuff's for babies," Blondie was saying. "Whyn't you and Olive Oyl come with me?" By *Olive Oyl* he meant me.

"Where?" Gretch wanted to know.

"A bunch of us get together under the boardwalk. Nobody down there to hassle us." He pried his shoulder away from

Madame Zaza's booth. "You comin'?" He walked out of the arcade.

I grabbed Gretchen's arm before her elbow dug into my ribs again. "Gretch, you've got to listen to me," I said through clenched teeth. "I'm sick!"

"Can't it wait? Kobie, he didn't mean anything by that Olive Oyl crack. Look, this is our last chance before we have to go home — "

"Haven't you heard a word I said? I'm *sick*! I can't take one step without throwing up!"

"You're just doing this to be spiteful, Kobie Roberts. If you don't come with me under the boardwalk, I'll never speak to you again." She meant it. And she wanted to go so badly, she couldn't see that under my sunburn my face was green.

"Go on, then. Find Blondie before he gets lost in the mob and wait for me by the bench across from here," I managed.

"What are you going to do?" she asked distractedly.

"You don't want to know." When Gretchen had left the arcade, I picked up a discarded paper cup that had once held french fries. Just in time. In full view of Madame Zaza and at least a hundred people, I retched into the cup. Then, as casually as if I threw up in public every day, I tossed the cup into a waste can and walked across the boardwalk with wobbly knees. Drinking in deep breaths of fresh air helped a little.

Blondie led the way down the steps and back under the boardwalk. Beneath the timbered braces twenty or so kids around our age or older were hidden in the shadows, laughing, sipping Cokes, boys horsing around with girls. At one glance I could see this gathering had nothing in common with that silly party I went to last year. These kids were way out of our league.

Gretchen turned to me, excited. "I'm going over to sit with Dwayne. Okay?"

"Who's Dwayne?"

"The guy we came down here with, dummy. Look, that boy over there is staring at you, Kobie." Of course he was staring. He'd probably never seen a green-faced toothpick before. Gretchen went over to Blondie and pretty soon he had his arm around her.

It was so easy for her — cute as she was, Gretchen would never have to worry about attracting guys. But then she'd had more practice at being thirteen than I'd had.

I found a splintery crate and sat down, drawing my knees up to my chin. Overhead, people clumped and clopped on the boards. I wondered how old the boardwalk was and how it could hold up, year after year, with so many people tramping its length.

Someone had a radio. When the strains of "Mr. Tambourine Man" began, a girl leaned over and switched up the volume. I let myself be carried away with the music, across the rumpled sands, out over the ocean to the pencil-line horizon where a barge moved steadily southward, like a toy being pulled by an unseen string.

"Take me for a trip upon your magic swirlin' ship . . ."

Day after tomorrow, we would go home, and next week, school would start. *This* year would be better, now that I was thirteen.

It just had to be.

Chapter 2

It was the ugliest dress in the history of humankind. It was also a hand-me-down, which hardly came as any revelation. The girl who owned it before me probably couldn't get it out of her closet fast enough. And I had to wear it on the first day of school.

"I *won't*," I announced to my mother. "You'll have to chloroform me to get me in that thing!"

"There is nothing wrong with that dress," my mother said. This was the same woman who also said there was nothing wrong with taking those hand-me-downs in the first place. "It's well-made and probably cost Dot a lot of money." Dot was my mother's friend. She claimed her daughter had grown too much to ever wear those clothes again but I knew the real truth:

Dot's daughter wouldn't be caught dead in them any more than I would.

"Can't I wear my skirt and sweater?" I whined. I had gotten one new back-to-school outfit, a plaid wool skirt and a blue cardigan sweater.

"Don't be ridiculous," my mother said. "It's going to be in the nineties today. Now get dressed before I smack you one."

End of discussion. I had no choice but to put on the ugly dress. Nobody at Robert Frost Junior High would be wearing anything so dreadful, I was certain. Made of some stiff, sturdy fabric, the dress was mud-pie brown, patterned with little yellow flowers. Plus it did all the wrong things for me. The too-wide neckline showed that my collarbone jutted out like a coat hanger, while the full skirt and babyish puffed sleeves made my legs and arms seem even skinnier.

"Don't you look pretty," my mother said, handing me my lunch money.

"That's right, I don't," I retorted as I stamped out the door to catch the bus.

Gretchen was already on the bus, in our special seat. She tried to hide her expression when she saw me.

"I look terrible, I know. If you want to pretend you never saw me before in your life, I'll understand." Close to tears, I stared glumly out the window.

Gretch and I had enough strikes against us in this school. Last year, when we were seventh-graders at Robert Frost, we had been treated like outcasts. Kids from several schools had been dumped into Frost and our little band from Centreville Elementary had been swallowed by hordes of these strange, new kids who ignored us.

We didn't live in ritzy Annandale, where they all lived, but in a stupid place out in the boonies called Willow Springs. Our fathers didn't work in nearby Washington, D.C., for the State Department, or on Capitol Hill or at the Pentagon, and our mothers didn't have cleaning ladies. Worse, we didn't have the right clothes, a factor that sealed our fate with a stamp of doom like nothing else. If you wore Bass Weejun loafers and a madras plaid shirt, you could join the in-crowd. Without those things, you might as well not exist. Last year, we didn't. This year Gretchen stood half a chance, but only if she wasn't seen associating with someone wearing the Ugliest Dress in the World.

Now Gretchen said soothingly, "It's not that bad, Kobie. Maybe you'll start a new fad and every girl in school will want a dress just like yours."

"Oh, sure. Well, let me tell you, the first kid who says she likes my dress can have it. I'll take it off right then and there and give it to her. I'd rather walk around in my slip." I noted that Gretchen wore a madras jumper in the latest style and brand-new loafers. "Weejuns?" I asked.

"No, but a good imitation." She smoothed the skirt of her jumper. "I hope it doesn't rain. If it rains on this dress, it's *ruined*."

Everybody who wore genuine madras got to say that. The cloth came from India or someplace and the plaid "bled" if it got wet, the colors running together. My dress was so stiff, I could have stood in the middle of a monsoon and it wouldn't even wrinkle. When my mother and I had gone school shopping, I had begged for a madras jumper, a madras blouse, even a madras purse. When Mom had read the label of an outrageously-priced A-line skirt, she had said indignantly, "Wash by hand in cold water only. How impractical for kids your age."

Gretchen tried to take my mind off my dress. "I hope we'll share a few classes."

"Fat chance. Last year we only had lunch together." It had been horrible, going through practically the whole day without my best friend. We had managed to give each other moral support during lunch, but it had still been tough.

"We won't know till we see our schedules," she said hopefully. "Keep your fingers crossed."

As the bus pulled into the unloading zone in front of the school, I was struck by the sea of madras pouring into the opened double doors. Nobody, but *nobody*, wore a dress that vaguely resembled mine. Like a condemned prisoner marching to the electric chair, I followed Gretchen into the hall and found that my homeroom was upstairs instead of downstairs like last year. I guess the teachers figured seventh graders were too klutzy to walk up the stairs. Gretchen was in a different homeroom so we planned to meet afterward.

I only recognized four kids from last year — Midge Murphy, who looked as if she had invented madras; Julia Neal, Midge's clone; Doug Peterson, who was born a hall monitor; and Richard Suppinger, whose only outstanding feature was his legendary ability to sleep through every single class without getting caught. Midge Murphy gave me the once-over as I passed her desk, but no one spoke to me.

Mrs. Shufflebarger, my homeroom teacher, didn't waste any time. She called the roll, passed out our schedules and medical forms, and assigned us lockers before Dr. Smyth, the principal, began his p.a. announcements. When the bell rang, I dashed out the door to find Gretchen.

"Who have you got for English?" she asked, as we compared schedules.

"Butler."

Gretchen whooped. "So do I!"

"But you have her in the afternoon. I've got her first period. What about American history? Who've you got?"

"Davis. Most of the kids in my homeroom have him."

My heart sank. "I've got Vandensomething or other. I can't even pronounce it. We don't have any classes together *again*!" I wailed. "What's the matter with this stupid school? Don't they realize they have to keep friends together or they'll *die*?"

"We have the same lunch period. That's better than nothing, Kobie. The bell's going to ring any second and I haven't found my locker yet. 'Bye! See you at noon!"

I had to locate my own locker. Number 1473 was near my first class, which was good. It was probably miles from all the others, though.

The shortest boy I had ever seen was twirling the combination lock of 1472. When I got closer, I saw he wore glasses and a look of steely determination, as if he dared me to say something about his height, or rather, the lack of it. Wearing the World's Ugliest Dress hardly entitled me to throw stones. I consulted the slip of paper with my combination on it and attempted to open my locker.

I hated those locks. They were built into the narrow metal door, just below the handle. You had to set the dial on exactly the right number or else it wouldn't open. And with three numbers — one to the left, one to the right, and back to the left again — it was easy to mess up. Also, you had to pass zero at least twice, humming the "Star-Spangled Banner," before it would open.

I would invariably spin the dial to the right, the left, and then the right. I'd finally sort out right from left by holding out my hands as an example (I'm right-handed) and start over, but then I'd forget about passing zero.

The kid next to me had his locker door open and was swinging it back and forth in my face, which did little to help my already scattered concentration.

"What's the matter?" he said, in a whiny kind of voice, as though he needed an adenoid operation. "Can't you open a simple little lock?"

"Of course," I returned tartly, whirling the dial recklessly in any old direction. "I just can't do it with you staring at me."

"Well, you're going to have to get used to that. My locker's right next to yours."

"So I noticed." Sweat was running down me and for once I was glad I didn't have on a madras dress, which would have undoubtedly bled under my arms. "Do you mind? You're in my light." That was a lie. Even if a five-zillion watt bulb had been suspended over my locker, I couldn't have gotten it open.

"Here. Let me show you." He took my locker combination from me.

"You can't see that! It's supposed to be confidential!"

"Do you want to get your locker open or not? We don't have all day." He read off my combination in a very loud, carrying voice. "Fifteen to the left! Seven to the right! Twenty-three to the left!"

"I'm glad you don't work for Fort Knox," I told him wryly. He lifted the handle of my locker and it opened. I leaned into the lovely, empty interior. At last the locker was mine! But I had just put my medical form on the high top shelf when he shoved me aside and slammed the door shut again.

"What'd you do that for?" I demanded. "I wasn't finished!"

"My name's Stuart Buckley," he said. "I'll send you a bill." Tucking my combination into his notebook, he hurried off down the hall.

"Hey! You've got my locker combination! Bring it back here, you little pipsqueak! I'm going to report you to the principal! I'll have you arrested for impersonating an eighth-grader!"

But he had disappeared in the crowd and the late bell was about to ring. I hustled to my first class, wondering what I had done to rate such a rat fink of a locker neighbor. It was probably the Curse of the Ugly Dress. Mrs. Shufflebarger had taken one look at it and had given me the locker next to Stuart Buckley's, figuring we deserved each other.

The day couldn't have gone downhill any faster if I had been pushed over Niagara Falls in a barrel.

My English teacher, who was young and pretty and was apparently offended by the color of mud-pie brown, assigned me a seat so far in the back of the room, I'd need binoculars to read the board and one of those old-fashioned ear trumpets to hear the lesson.

Mrs. Humphrey, my home ec teacher, had already decided on our sewing project: a shirtwaist dress with a collar and cuffs, tucks down the front, a buttoned placket, and a side-seam zipper. The next hardest project she could have dreamed up for us to make would have been a space suit.

One second after algebra class started, I realized I was sunk. Since I had learned almost nothing in math last year, I don't know why I thought algebra would be any easier.

And at lunchtime, I found Gretchen sitting with a bunch of girls from her phys. ed. class.

"Kobie, this is Julia Neal, and Midge Murphy, and that's Carol Hubbard. Sit down. The pizza is positively revolting."

I sat across from Midge in the only available chair and flashed Gretchen a look. We were supposed to compare notes at lunch. How could I complain with these other girls around?

Julia was saying, "They have pizza the first day every year, I guess to make us think the lunches are going to be edible."

"I heard all the cafeteria ladies saved up their scabs all summer to use as the crust," I volunteered. I had heard no such thing, naturally, but it certainly spiced up the conversation.

"Gross!" Julia cried and the others squealed.

"It's their way of getting back at us for sticking gum under the chairs," I continued breezily. I bit into my slice of pizza with zest, to show them I never let anything as trivial as a scab hinder my appetite.

When we carried our trays to the counter, Gretchen hissed, "What's the matter with you, Kobie? Talking about scabs while we're trying to eat!"

"I wanted them to leave. I had all kinds of stuff to tell you and I couldn't do it with them sitting there."

"Why not?"

"Because —" I searched my brain for a good reason. "Because you're my best friend, that's why. You should be there when I need you. Not hanging around with those snobs."

"They're not snobs. Julia is very nice. I'll admit Midge is a little stuck-up, but —"

"I don't care about Midge Murphy!" I cried. "Lunch is over and I haven't been able to tell you one word about my disastrous morning. I might as well have eaten with Stuart Buckley!"

"Who?"

"This pipsqueak who stole my locker

combination, that's who." Before I could explain further, the bell shrilled and lunch was over.

"I'll see you on the bus," Gretchen called, as she ran to catch up with her new friends.

I threw my trash in the can, slung my tray on the counter, and ran to my next class.

In phys. ed., Miss Compton measured and weighed us, then made us sit on the floor and take off our shoes so she could examine our feet, checking to see if any of us had athlete's foot. After that humiliation, she informed us a new gym suit style was available for those who had outgrown last year's. The well-cut shorts and camp shirt were a big improvement over the despised one-piece bloomer suit. Everybody but me clustered around Miss Compton's assistant, putting in their orders. Since my growth had stalled at five foot three, eighty-four pounds, I could count on being *married* in my one-piece bloomer suit. Miss Compton also told us field hockey would start the next day and my shins ached at the thought. Some of those girls were wicked with a hockey stick in their hands.

My history teacher was a tall, big-boned

woman with grayish hair indifferently whacked off just below her earlobes and black-rimmed glasses. She wore a black turtleneck and a black wool skirt, as hot as it was. She greeted us with the information that anyone who couldn't spell or pronounce her name correctly would automatically flunk her course. Then she wrote her name on the board and it was a lulu: Eteska Vandenheuvel. I scribbled it on the back of my schedule, resolving to commit it to memory before I went to bed.

My last class of the day was art, my favorite subject, and I was delighted Mrs. Ryerson was my teacher again. I'd had her in seventh grade and just loved her. She seemed glad to have me back in her class and asked me if I had done any drawing over the summer. I had exciting news to tell her, but decided to wait until another day, when the place wasn't such a madhouse.

When the bell rang, I realized I had left my medical form in my locker. My homeroom teacher had made such a big point of getting those forms in immediately, I pictured her giving me a stern lecture if I didn't bring mine in tomorrow. But Stuart Buckley had my locker combination! He was probably at his locker — I'd just make the little weasel give it back to me.

Sure enough, he was standing in front of 1472, whistling.

"You ran off with my locker combination," I accused. "I want it back this instant!"

"Instead of flapping your gums, why don't you try to open your locker?" he said.

"How can I without the combination?" Then I noticed the door was open slightly. I yanked it open and there, inside, was the form and the paper with my locker combination. I reached for them, but before I had my arm all the way out, Stuart slammed the door shut on me. "Hey!" I yelled in surprise.

He shot through the crowd as if he were on jet-propelled roller skates. I rubbed my sore arm, silently calling Stuart Buckley the worst possible names I could think of.

Gretchen had reserved our special seat on the bus. "Well, how was it?"

A few hours ago I'd been dying to dump my miseries on someone. Now all I wanted to do was close my eyes and shut out the world. "Don't ask."

My mother was waiting for me at home, bright-eyed over her only daughter's first day of eighth grade. "Tell me about your day. How was school?"

"Wonderful." I threw the medical form

on the kitchen table, grabbed a Twinkie from the bread box, unplugged the radio sitting on the yellow tea cart, and went into my room. I would fill her in on all the gory details at dinner, but I had to be alone for a while.

I set the radio on my dresser and moved the dial from my parent's twangy country music station to WPGC. Cousin Duffy, the d.j., was spouting some nonsense as the lead-in to the next record. Then a new song by the Beach Boys began playing and I felt myself relaxing. I had listened to the radio every night since I had gotten back from Ocean City and I knew the Top 40 as well as Gretchen. I loved Sonny and Cher and the Beach Boys and the Beatles and, of course, the Byrds. I wished I had a record player so I could play "Mr. Tambourine Man" as many times as I wanted, instead of having to rely on the whims of Cousin Duffy.

I ate half my Twinkie, then put the un-eaten half on the nightstand. It would leave a greasy little Twinkie track and my mother would yell, but I didn't care. After a day like today, nothing she could say would make me feel any worse.

Lying back on my pillows, I reviewed my situation. It was, in a word, cruddy. Gretchen had a new madras jumper and fake Weejun loafers and three new friends. I had a dress that even an orphan would scorn, a shrimp who slammed my locker shut, and no friends, except for Gretchen, and I suspected she was moving on to greener pastures.

I had a secret, though.

Reaching under my bed, I pulled out a cardboard shirt box. Inside the box was my future, my ticket to fame and glory. Let all those finks at Robert Frost have their fun.

"When I'm rich and famous they'll be sorry they didn't treat me better," I said aloud, enjoying the warm, satisfying picture of Midge Murphy pleading to be my friend when she discovered I'd become a Big Wheel in Hollywood. Anticipating revenge made me feel gooshy inside, like the cream filling in my Twinkie.

I lifted the lid of the box and took out a pile of drawings and a typewritten letter. The letter was from Walt Disney Productions, way out in Burbank, California. It said they were happy to receive my letter asking them for a job, but that animators at Walt Disney Studios were required to take special training, even after graduating from art school. Okay, so they figured out I was just a kid, but Mr. Disney's secretary or whoever wrote the letter told me the pictures I sent them were very good and I shouldn't be discouraged.

I supposed I'd have to wait a few years before I could apply there again, but in the meantime, I planned to work on my drawing.

There's not a whole lot to do in Willow Springs, anyway. With no brothers or sisters around, or any friends who lived nearby (Gretch's house was five miles away), I drew pictures to pass the time. Drawing was the most important thing in the world to me, especially since the *Life* magazine story.

One day last year when I was waiting in the dentist's office, I had found a story about Walt Disney's animation studio. There were color pictures taken from the cartoon movies, like *Snow White, Cinderella*, and *Sleeping Beauty*. I had seen all those movies and loved them. But this article showed the people who made the pictures. Animators, they were called. They drew the figures over painted backgrounds and made them move with a special camera.

I hadn't been able to read the whole thing before my turn came, so I had ripped the story out of the magazine and stuffed it in my pocket when the receptionist wasn't looking. I figured it was the least Dr. O'Brian owed me, since he managed to kill me every time I got in his chair.

Later, I had tried copying some of the movie scenes, which were painted on cels, according to the article. It was a lot harder than it looked. I had done one picture over eight times. Then I dragged out all my old Donald Duck comic books and started drawing those pictures, too. The way I saw it, if I got a job at Walt Disney Studios, they'd put me to work on cartoons first, instead of the full-length animated movies, so I'd better bone up on my Donald Duck. But even if they had me sweeping the floor, at least I'd actually be in that studio, watching others make those wonderful pictures. That was my dream.

Now I set the letter aside and took out my latest drawing. I frowned. It was good, but not good enough. My biggest problem was coloring the drawing. I had drawn a scene from *Cinderella*, where two mice struggled to carry a huge key up an enormous marble staircase. I had sketched the mice in pencil first, then went over the outlines with laundry ink. I had finished coloring the mice and had started working on the steps. My crayons just weren't right. The picture in the magazine showed the steps in soft browns and grays with shadows falling from above. My version looked too crayon-y.

The animators used special inks and paints. All I had was a box of Crayolas, the sixty-four size. They would have to do.

Something in the expression of the pointy-faced mouse, pushing the heavy brass key up to his buddy on the steps above, made me study the picture more closely. Was it my imagination, or did he look like Stuart Buckley? He did. If Stuart had whiskers and a pink blob on the end of his nose, he could trade places with this mouse. I wished he *would* trade places with a mouse — then he wouldn't be able to slam my locker door shut.

I doodled a pair of glasses on my mouse, wondering how I was going to keep the real-life little rat from driving me crazy.

Chapter 3

Before I left for school the next morning,
I went through my Disney drawings and
picked out six of my best. One in particular, of Donald Duck riding a flying carpet,
was especially good, I thought. If Mrs.
Ryerson, my art teacher, wasn't too busy,
I would show them to her and maybe she
would — well, I didn't know what she'd do,
but packing my drawings in the blue
plastic insurance envelope I used for a portfolio made facing the day a little easier.

Gretchen moved over to make room for
me when I got on the bus. "Hi," she mur-
mured.

"Hi." I sat down, setting my notebook
and portfolio in my lap. Then I noticed she
was wearing stockings. Real nylon hose,
not tights.

She stretched out one stockinged leg for
me to admire. "I finally talked my mother

into letting me wear them. No more baby-ish knee socks for me."

As one who happened to be wearing babyish knee socks, I couldn't think of anything to say, except, "What color are they?"

"It's called 'Cinnamon.' People's brand," she replied, matter-of-factly.

If I hadn't liked Gretchen so much, I probably would have hated her at that moment. She didn't act smug about her graduation from socks to stockings, or try to rub it in. But we both knew she had taken one more step ahead of me. I felt frumpy and childish sitting next to her, with my knobby knees sticking out above my white cotton knee socks.

"I prefer 'Coffee' myself," I said. My mother happened to wear that shade. The more I thought about my mother and Gretch's new stockings, the more I realized it was all my mother's fault I was being held back.

As usual, Gretch read my mind. "When do you think your mom will let you wear hose?"

I sighed wearily. "Probably never. I'm surprised she ever let me out of diapers." The sad truth was, my mother planned to keep me in knee socks until I was thirty-five. I had a very disturbing image of myself at that age in a black dress and pearls and pink knee socks.

"Maybe my mom can talk to yours," Gretchen suggested helpfully, absently pushing back her shiny hair. In all fairness, I don't think Gretch liked wearing hose before I did. After all, we'd been friends for most of our natural lives and it was probably pretty scary becoming an adult. It wasn't a process I would choose to go through without my best friend.

"Forget it," I told her. "If your mother tells mine you're wearing stockings, that'll probably throw my mother in reverse. She'll have me back in booties." I shifted the things in my lap.

Gretchen saw my portfolio but said nothing. She never raved over my drawings the way some people did. (Okay, so my fans were limited to aging relatives and drop-in company who were too polite to say anything else when forced to admire my artwork.) The most Gretch had ever done was admit I could draw well, while she couldn't draw a straight line with a ruler. That was cool. I mean, I didn't need to have my best friend gushing every five minutes about what a great artist I was. Did I thank Edison every time I turned on a light switch?

"What clubs are you joining?" Gretchen wanted to know.

"None. I hate clubs," I answered sullenly. I've despised organized activity ever since third grade when I attended a Brownie meeting. I thought the other kids looked stupid in their chocolate-milk-colored uniforms and only went in the first place because I'd heard there would be cupcakes and punch.

"That's your trouble, Kobie. You need to get into the groove, do what everybody else is doing. You don't want to be an outcast forever, do you?"

I looked at her. "And this is your way of becoming an incast — joining all those dumb clubs."

"They aren't all dumb. I'm joining Drama. Julia says it's a lot of fun. And Midge thinks I ought to run for Student Council. What do you think?"

I didn't tell Gretch what I really thought — she'd never speak to me again. If Midge Murphy and Julia Neal had already convinced Gretch to do those things, then nothing I could say would make any difference.

Gretchen rattled on, her blue eyes bright. "If we're going to change this year, Kobie, we have to play the game *their* way. Go to meetings and stuff, even if they don't seem like much fun. What you ought to do is get the list of after-school groups from your homeroom teacher and sign up for one. It's a way in."

I stared out the window, wondering if there was a club for people with wretched lives and ugly clothes. If there was, I would have been a charter member. "I don't think so. It's just not for me. You run for Student Council. I'll make your campaign posters, how's that?"

"Great. Midge called me last night with some cute campaign slogans. You can draw pictures to fit the slogans."

Wonderful. Now my artistic talents were going to be used to illustrate "A vote for Gretchen is a vote for the best o'them," or some such drivel. "Is Midge going to be your campaign manager?" I asked.

"I hope so. She was S.C. secretary last year, so she knows the ropes."

One more area of Gretchen's life I had been squeezed out of. "Fine," I said tightly. "I'll do your posters if Midge provides the poster paper and paints. I don't have the money for that kind of stuff, you know."

"Speaking of posters," Gretchen said, "did you see the one about the school dances? It was on the eighth-grade bulletin board."

I shook my head. With Stuart Buckley

slamming my locker every other minute, I hadn't seen anything yesterday except black spots of rage. "What dances?"

"Fridays after school. Starting this Friday. You don't have to have a date. Just show up. They're called mixers."

"And what do they mix?"

Gretchen laughed. "Boys with girls, dummy. What did you think?"

So Gretch knew about such sophisticated things as mixers. Midge Murphy had probably told her on the phone last night. After they had discussed Gretchen's S.C. campaign. And after deciding what color stockings to wear the next day.

I didn't get a chance to show Mrs. Ryerson my Disney drawings. She announced our first project would be working with modeling clay, and proceeded to scoop out big lumps of the putty-colored stuff from a tub, as each kid went up and got his share.

I wasn't crazy about the idea of making something from clay. For one thing, I hated to get my hands in it. In fact, I didn't really like any other aspect of art except drawing, not even painting. I tended to hold the paintbrush like a pen and draw with it, which you aren't supposed to do. Most of the other kids loved sloppy projects, like fooling around with clay, or gobbing oil on a canvas, or tearing up magazines to make a collage. To me, that wasn't art. I wanted to be left alone with my paper and ink and when I was finished, I would have a precise, finely-etched drawing of something you could *recognize*, not some papier-maché blob painted orange and purple.

The clay Mrs. Ryerson put into my cupped hands looked alarmingly like a brain and even felt about the same size. I took my clay back to my plastic-swathed table and waited for the teacher's instructions.

"The first thing you must do," she told the class, "is pound the clay. Pound it on the table like this." She hefted a wad of clay over her head and threw it on the table in front of her with a loud *thwack*. "Over and over again. You have to get the air bubbles out of your clay before you can even think about modeling it. We're going to fire your sculptures in the kiln and then glaze them. If there is an air bubble left in your statue, it could explode." As she spoke, she kept throwing her clay against the table.

"How many times do we have to do this?" a kid asked.

"At least four class sessions," she replied. "Now get busy pounding." She took off her apron and left the room. Approximately one second later, I knew why.

Have you ever heard thirty kids throwing brain-sized lumps of clay against hard surfaces? By comparison, a stampede of buffalo sounds as quiet as a mouse muffled in cotton.

After nine or ten throws, I began to develop a rhythm. Pick up clay, hold over head, throw. Pick up, hold over head, throw. It really wasn't such a bad way to end my second day as an eighth-grader. Maybe when I grew up, I could get a job doing something this menial and mindless, like turning the same knob over and over. What other job could I *expect* to be hired for, wearing knee socks?

Pick up, hold over head, throw. My shins still hurt from the battling I'd received in field hockey earlier that day. I knew my kneecaps were knobby, but surely those girls could tell human legs from a hockey puck.

Gym had been bad enough, but home ec had been even worse. We had practiced laying the pattern pieces for the shirtwaist dresses we were supposed to make on a sample length of fabric. There must have been three dozen pieces. When I had complained I'd never seen a dress with five sleeves and three collars, Mrs. Humphrey had not been amused. She'd retaliated by handing out a mimeographed list of the sewing supplies we would have to buy, in addition to the four hundred or so yards of material it would take to make the dress. My mother wasn't going to like that part one bit. She claimed it cost more and more to send me to school each year. At this point, I would gladly volunteer to quit to save her and Daddy the money.

In history, Mrs. Vandenheuvel had told us — commanded, really — we would have to take *very good* notes in *every single* class and keep these notes in a notebook that she would grade at the end of the quarter. We ought to start preparing ourselves for college, she had said. Apparently, college teachers don't repeat things, and they don't write things on the blackboard, and they speak very fast while they stroll around the room, adjusting the blinds or eating cherry Lifesavers.

Mrs. Vandenheuvel had also showed us some shorthand symbols of common words like "that," "and," "America," and so on to make note-taking speedier because that's the way they do it in college. I had made a mental note to apply only to schools in the deep South, when the time came, where they talked even slower than they do in

Virginia, as I had scribbled, "The Crusades blank travels blank blank Polo's made people wish blank find blank route blank blank riches blank blank East." I planned to fill in the blanks with the appropriate shorthand symbols later.

At the end of class, Mrs. Vandenheuvel had passed around a "Peanuts" cartoon clipped from that day's *Washington Post*. I'd thought that was a nice touch, even though my fingers had been too cramped from furious note-taking to hold it.

Now it felt good to throw a hunk of clay. My fingers gradually loosened from claws back to their normal state. As I pounded my clay, I pretended I was hitting, with each throw, my algebra teacher, who seemed determined that I at least learn how to *spell* the word *algebra* even if I didn't accomplish another thing in his class; Mrs. Vandenheuvel and her shorthand version of the Crusades; Mrs. Humphrey with her darts and basting stitches, and good old Stuart Buckley, who had managed to slam my locker shut twice that day. Take that, and that, and that!

Mrs. Ryerson hadn't been kidding when she'd said we'd have to pound our clay four whole class sessions. On the fifth day, she let us begin making whatever we wanted with the clay. I decided against a lopsided ashtray or a pin dish, like a lot of the others were making, and sculpted a cat, somewhat like an Egyptian statue. It turned out pretty well, even if one side of the cat's face drooped a little. I planned to give it to my mother for Christmas, the lucky woman.

Our statues went into the kiln in bunches, which Mrs. Ryerson fired when we weren't there. A few days later, I entered the art room to see our statues, now white from baking, and the glazes lined up on the counter for us to use. Among the ashtrays and pin dishes that resembled fried eggs, I could not find my Egyptian cat.

"Where's mine?" I asked Mrs. Ryerson.

She clucked her tongue and shook her head sadly. "I'm afraid we had a little accident in the kiln yesterday. Someone — not you, Kobie, dear — did not pound out all his bubbles. His statue exploded and hit yours, which was next to it."

"My cat broke?" I said unbelievingly.

"I'm afraid so. It wasn't as bad as it could have been," she said, producing my cat from a shelf in the supply cupboard. "Its tail came off and I took the liberty of gluing it back on. See? Once you glaze it, nobody will know the difference."

I would, I wanted to cry indignantly. I took my poor wounded cat and asked, "Who didn't get all his bubbles out?"

"Someone from another class. His name is Stuart Buckley."

Before Stuart could slam my locker, I grabbed his wrist. "What's the idea of ruining my cat? Why didn't you pound out all your bubbles like the rest of us?"

"What are you babbling about?" he said, yanking his arm free.

"My cat statue. Your statue blew up in the kiln and broke mine. Can't you leave me alone *anywhere*?"

"Boy!" He twirled his finger next to his temple. "You've really cracked."

"I have not cracked! I worked very hard on my cat statue. It was my mother's Christmas present. Now I have to give her a cat with a glued-on tail! That's the whole idea of making a sculpture — it's supposed to be all in one piece. Mine was the *only one* ruined in six art classes. *Mine*! And *you* did it!"

Stuart shrugged. "Sorry. My statue blew to smithereens. Big deal, it was dumb-looking, anyway."

"Why did *yours* have to be next to *mine*? Just like this stupid locker!" I pulled out the books I needed for homework.

Stuart saw the blue plastic insurance envelope that held my drawings. Since I hadn't gotten a chance to show them to my art teacher, I had put the portfolio in my locker. "What's this?" he said, reaching for the envelope. "You selling insurance?"

"Leave that alone!" I smacked his hand, but the envelope fell out, spilling my drawings all over the floor.

Stuart picked up my Donald Duck on the magic carpet, hooting. "Get a load of this! Donald Duck! Hey, did you see this? Look what Kobie drew! Isn't it cute? Hey, Kobie, where's Mickey Mouse?"

A group had gathered, snickering at my pictures. I snatched up the spilled drawings and stuffed them back in the envelope, my face burning. Darn that Stuart! He was going to destroy my entire life, no two ways about it.

Maybe Gretchen was right. Maybe I ought to stop fighting the system and get into things. If I didn't, I doubted I would live to see fourteen.

Chapter 4

Gretchen appointed herself as a combination coach/fairy godmother to help in my transformation. On the phone after school we plotted my launch into the in-crowd. "We'll go to one of those dances and I'll introduce you to some kids," she said. "You'll have a great time. Trust me." Gretchen had already been to three of the Friday mixers, so she was an authority on the subject.

"What if a boy asks me to dance?" I asked.

"You *dance* with him, silly! Unless he's a creep and you don't want to."

"What if a boy *doesn't* ask me to dance?"

She didn't answer. Undoubtedly, she had never encountered that particular situation. Gretchen was vice-president of the eighth grade, and her popularity at Frost had soared to skyscraper heights. My own popularity, which had always hovered somewhere around basement level, had nose-dived to subterranean depths after the spilled-drawing incident.

"The important thing," Gretchen emphasized, "is that you get in there and fight. Stand up and be noticed."

"People notice me all right," I replied sourly. "But for the wrong things." Weeks after Stuart had flashed my drawings in the hall, kids still teased me about my Mickey Mouse pictures.

"They'll forget about that, as soon as they see what a great dancer you are," Gretchen said stoutly, overlooking the fact that I *wasn't* a great dancer. I didn't even qualify as a *bad* dancer. I couldn't dance a step, not counting the swaying I did in the privacy of my bedroom when "Mr. Tambourine Man" came on the radio.

"There's nothing to dancing," Gretchen insisted when I pointed this out to her. "Just jump around like everybody else. You're always so worried about what people think of you, Kobie. If you'd get involved in things, you wouldn't dwell on yourself so much. Where's your team spirit?"

Spending so much time with Midge Murphy, Gretchen had developed a tendency to speak in Cheerleader-ese. If her next words were "Two, four, six, eight, who do we appreciate?" I planned to hang up on her.

Instead she surprised me by saying, "You really ought to get a new outfit, Kobie. Having something new to wear to the dance will bolster your confidence."

"What confidence?" I tossed back, but she was right. Now all I had to do was convince my mother that if I didn't have an outfit exactly like all the other girls were wearing, I had no reason to go on living.

Friday night was bank- and grocery-night. My father got paid from his job as foreman of the Grounds Department of the county schools, so it was the most exciting night of the entire week.

I sat in the back seat of our dumpy old Chevrolet, humming "Mr. Tambourine Man" to myself, while my parents talked over mundane grown-up matters as Daddy drove us to Manassas. There was a familiarity about this ritual, repeated faithfully every week, that made me feel warm and content.

My mother sat just in front of me, wearing her brown checked bank-night dress, her big black pocketbook resting on the seat between her and my father. As she talked, she absently opened and closed the chunky gold clasp, a thick, clunk-clunk sound I found oddly pleasant. Sometimes it was nice to fall back into the old, comfortable role of a little kid.

Too bad it wouldn't last. What my mother didn't know, as she discussed with Daddy whether or not to get a ham, was that this week the routine was going to be different. Very different.

We drove down Lee Highway to the town of Centreville, which we passed in a wink. Daddy turned off on to Route 28. As we approached the top of the long grade, I watched for the first glimpse of the distant Blue Ridge Mountains, purple with dusk, marching north to south in an unbroken chain like a parade of elephants. Seeing the mountains always made me feel exhilarated, as if I were on the verge of discovering something important.

The road was dark, a long black ribbon laced with telephone wires. I crossed my fingers when we bumped over the bridge spanning the Bull Run River, a holdover from when I was younger and afraid we wouldn't make it to the other side.

After so much unrelieved darkness, Manassas burst upon us in a festival of lights and neon signs like fireworks at a Fourth of July picnic. Daddy pulled into the parking lot of the shopping center and

I jumped out of the car before it stopped rolling and had to be called back. I meekly swallowed the chewing-out my father gave me, realizing this was no way to start off my mission. I followed my mother into the bank and then the grocery store, while Daddy waited in the car. We carried four sacks of groceries to the car, then my mother and I went into Peeble's department store. Zero hour had arrived.

I saw the outfit in the Young Junior section of the store right away. A mannequin modeled the latest style from Carnaby Street in London— a blue hip-hugger miniskirt, a ribbed "poor boy" top, and wild patterned tights. Midge Murphy and Julia Neal had already worn miniskirts and poor boys to school and the other girls were copying them fast.

My mother was heading to the back of the store to the underwear department, giving me about three seconds to nail her attention.

"Oh, Mom, look!" I shrieked. "Isn't that the *cutest* outfit you've ever seen! Right there, see it? Oh, Mom, I just *love* it! Can I have it, can I, can I, please?"

My mother stopped in her tracks and turned around to stare at me as if she'd never seen me before. She probably wished she hadn't. At least half the people in the

store were gawking at us. Begging on grocery night — or any other night, for that
matter — was forbidden on pain of death.
Once, when I was little, I'd thrown a fit
for a box of Dreamsicles, and had been
immediately rewarded with a smack and
the strong warning that I was never to do
that again. If I wanted something, I would
ask for it in a reasonable tone, and if I
couldn't have it, that would be the end of it.

However, tonight I had too much at stake
to follow the rules. I knew what my
mother's arguments would be if I asked
reasonably for a new outfit. "I didn't come
in this store to buy you clothes, Kobie" or
"We don't have the money for such foolish-
ness." She always said stuff like that,
which was why I had to resort to drastic
measures to catch her off guard.

It worked, sort of. "What?" she said in
a dazed voice.

"This outfit, I have to have it!" I pointed
at the mannequin like somebody who had
gone berserk. "There's a dance next Friday
and I want to wear this to it. Will you buy
it for me, Mama, please, please? Pretty
please with sugar on it?"

"Kobie, for heaven's sake, what's gotten
into you? You know we don't have the
money for new clothes tonight."

"You *always* say that! We never have

enough money for anything," I wailed. "Everybody gets new things but me! I have to wear the same old rags day in and day out."

Now my mother tugged the price tags into view, then stuffed them back, her lips thinned. "We simply can't afford this, Kobie. I'm sorry."

I wasn't about to give up that easily. "Buy it for me for Christmas! I won't ask for another thing, I promise."

"I've already bought your Christmas present," she argued.

"Take it back! Whatever it is, I don't want it. I want *this*!" I hurled myself at the mannequin's feet, nearly chipping a front tooth on the stupid thing's plaster shinbone.

My mother was mortified. "Kobie, get up this instant!" she said in a dangerous tone. When I got up, my face suitably tear-streaked, she sighed and examined the skirt. "This isn't worth the money. I can make you one a lot cheaper."

"Can you do it by next Friday? And will it be blue corduroy like this one?"

"I have some green corduroy at home. It'll do just fine."

I remembered the fabric in her sewing chest, the color of army fatigues. "Let's buy some material here," I urged her.

"I spent enough on fabric for your home ec project," she countered. "If you want the skirt, it'll have to be green."

I conceded the point to her. An ugly-colored miniskirt was better than none.

We went to Woolworth's to find a pattern. I picked out a wide, curved hip-hugger belt to go with my skirt, while my mother sorted through some tops that were on sale.

"Here's a nice knit top," she said.

I glanced disdainfully at the purple flowered monstrosity she held up. "I can't wear that with my miniskirt. I have to wear a poor boy top with it."

"And why do you have to wear that exact top?" she wanted to know.

"Because. That's what *everybody's* wearing. Can we go back to Peeble's and buy one?"

"No." She rooted around and came up with a rust-colored cotton imitation of a poor boy. "This will do, won't it?"

With the extreme tips of my fingers, I held the cheap ribbed top at arm's length, as if it were crawling with maggots. "I guess so. But I *have* to have patterned tights. The whole outfit will look awful if I have to wear knee socks." For once, luck was on my side. I found a pair of hunter green and rust tights in a diamond design that was perfect.

Our next stop was Drug Fair. While my mother had a prescription filled at the pharmacy, I strolled around the makeup section. There was a big display of Yardley cosmetics, marked by a huge photograph of one of those English models with heavy-lidded smoldering eyes and pale, chalky lips. All the girls at Frost had the Yardley look. Midge Murphy pulled her Yardley lipstick out of her purse at least five times at lunch. I longed for one of those ringed metal tubes to carry in my purse.

I was all ready for my mother when she located me. Pointing to the display, I squealed, "Oh, Mama, look! Everybody wears Yardley makeup. Can I have a lipstick and maybe a little eye shadow? Please, please, please?"

My mother squinted disapprovingly at the poster. "Absolutely not. That stuff is much too old for you. Look at that girl's eyelids — she must have laid that goop on with a trowel. And her mouth — whoever heard of blue lipstick! Kobie, I think your generation has lost its mind, wanting to look like that."

"You never want me to look pretty!" I shrieked. "No wonder I don't have any friends. I'm the ugliest girl in school and it's all your fault! I look like those girls in the prison movies — all I need is one of those horrible gray dresses!"

"Kobie, I'm not putting up with this. I've already spent more on you than I intended. Where do you think the money comes from? You think it grows on trees? I'm leaving the store, right now." She marched off down the aisle.

I stood firm, not budging from the Yardley display. My mother stalked back a moment later, her eyes blazing.

"Are you coming with me, young lady, or not?" she demanded.

I folded my arms across my chest, digging in for a long siege. "Not. I'm not going anywhere until you let me buy some make-up."

"Your father is waiting for us. Do you want me to go out to the car and bring him in? If I have to, I will. You know he won't be so patient with your childish behavior." She took a step away. "I'm going, Kobie. If you don't come on, I'm going to get him."

Believe me, this was not fun. Suddenly I felt a twinge for the old days when my mother gave me a quarter every Friday to spend in Drug Fair. I would buy a *Little Lulu* comic and a pack of chewing gum and be happy as a clam. In those days I didn't care if I went out the door wearing fishing boots and my father's old bathrobe, and I thought makeup was the ickiest stuff in the world. Being thirteen was no bed of roses.

My mother heaved a sigh. "I don't know what's gotten into you lately, Kobie Roberts, but I'm ready to ship you off to reform school. All right. You can have a lipstick but not that blue stuff." She pulled a plain, clear lip gloss from the rack. "This is more suitable for a girl your age."

I took the lip gloss and the dollar she handed me up to the checkout counter, happy I now had one of those distinctive ringed tubes to pull out of my purse at lunchtime. While I waited in line, I mentally tallied my purchases: a hip-hugger belt, lip gloss, patterned hose, a facsimile of a poor boy top, and the promise of a miniskirt by next Friday. Mission accomplished.

My mother stood a little apart from me, clutching her black plastic pocketbook and the prescription bag, and looking as if she wished she had switched babies in the hospital. I turned away, feeling a gritty sort of triumph that I had made her buy all those things she hadn't intended. I had a certain power over her, I realized for the first time. I also felt that an invisible barrier had suddenly sprung up between us and that we would be on opposite sides for a long time.

I was third in line when I saw the record display, propped on a counter. And right in front was the Byrds' new album, *Mr. Tambourine Man.* Something inside my chest squeezed so I could hardly breathe. There was my song! And with a picture of the group who sang it!

Sucking in a gulp of air strong enough to strip the shelves of aspirin bottles, I screeched, "Mom! Look! There's my *Mr. Tambourine Man* record! Oh, Mom, I have to have it! Can I get it, can I, can I, please?" I heard a sharp, desperate edge in my own voice that hadn't been there even when I was pleading for the miniskirt. "Mr. Tambourine Man" made me do things like that.

My mother came over and examined the record, looking at the price tag. "But Kobie, we don't even have a record player."

"I don't care! I don't need a record player. I just want to have the record! Please, Mom, please, it means everything in the whole world to own this record!" I was practically sobbing.

The other two people ahead of me in line and the guy running the cash register were staring at us. What was left of my mother's patience crumbled. Thrusting three wadded bills in my hand, she said, "Get the record. Get anything you want. But I'd better not hear another *peep* out of you for the next month, is that clear?"

I nodded, nearly fainting with happiness, and bought my precious record.

I thought Mom would tell Daddy about my revolting behavior in the shopping center, but she never said a word. At home, my mother went to her room where she counted out the week's money and sorted the bills into little piles. She gave me a black look as I passed her door, and I knew she would have to borrow from her emergency fund to make up what she had spent on me tonight.

In my room, I closed the door and laid my purchases on my bed. I stared at the cover of my album, memorizing the photograph of the five guys who called themselves the Byrds. I didn't even tear off the shrink-wrap plastic, afraid that some of the magic from *Mr. Tambourine Man* might leak out.

Chapter 5

On the day before the dance, I came home from school to find my mother had finished my new miniskirt. It lay on my bed, freshly pressed. I tried on my new outfit, then went into my parents' room to see myself in the full-length mirror hanging on the back of the closet door.

The hip-hugger belt fit snugly over my hipbones and the wild patterned tights made my legs look less skinny. I almost looked like one of those stick-thin English models who were in all the fashion magazines.

My mother twitched at the hem of my skirt. "It's so short, Kobie. But I guess it's supposed to be. You look real cute."

"Except for my hair," I groaned. Suddenly I wanted hair like Midge Murphy's, shining clean and falling from a ruler-straight part with the ends just curving under my chin.

"Your hair is fine," my mother said.

"It is *not*. It's *horrible*!"

"Well, I could trim your bangs," she suggested.

"You're not touching my bangs," I told her quickly. We had a long-standing feud about my bangs. Every year, the day before my school picture was taken, my mother would trim my bangs, using old notched scissors that had last been used for cutting asphalt shingles or something equally dulling. As a result, my bangs would be about a half an inch long and there I'd be with all that face hanging out. No wonder my school pictures were so ghastly.

"If you don't want your bangs trimmed, I don't know what you're complaining about," my mother said, exasperated.

"*You* wouldn't understand. You only want me to look ugly!"

Her temper flared. "Okay, you're ugly! *Now* are you happy? I don't know what's the matter with you, Kobie. I can't do or say anything right these days."

Instead of answering her, I locked myself in the bathroom. My mother kept her hair rollers on a shelf and I decided to help myself. I also found something called

Comb 'N Set. It was setting lotion, a clear, thick liquid the consistency of molasses that was supposed to make hair shiny, soft, and manageable. I slathered Comb 'N Set liberally over my hair, set it, then got under the hair dryer. After supper, I ran into the bathroom, eager to take the rollers out and have beautiful hair just like Midge Murphy. I would be the hit of the dance.

The setting lotion had made my hair shiny, all right, more like varnished, and I soon discovered the only way I could manage it was with a whip and chair. I couldn't even comb it — my hair was so stiff, teeth flew off the comb like popcorn and my hairbrush dragged through the curls like a chainsaw balking through a log. Even worse, each curl had a bump where the snap-on cover held the roller in place, so the curls sproinged in all the wrong directions.

With tears streaming down my cheeks, I tied my hideous curls back with a ribbon, then went to bed, wishing I had never let Gretchen talk me into going to that stupid dance.

The dance was held in the cafetorium, the huge room that was a combination cafeteria and auditorium. At one end was an elaborate stage with velvet curtains and loudspeakers, while the rest of the room looked like a cafeteria. During assemblies, the long lunch tables were moved to the back and chairs were arranged in rows in front of the stage.

Today, the lunch tables were piled under the windows at one end and the chairs lined the walls. Music blared from the loud-speakers. I hung back in the doorway, thinking if I hurried I might still have time to catch my regular bus home. Just then Gretchen spotted me and left a group of kids to come get me.

"Come on," she said, drawing me into the room. "I want you to meet Jake and Carrie and some of the others."

"Gretchen, I'm not sure I want to —"

"Stop it, Kobie. You're here to have fun. Give it a chance." We had reached Gretchen's circle of admirers. She thrust me into the group. "Everybody, this is Kobie. Kobie, that's Jake, and that's Carrie. You know Midge and Julia."

The girl called Carrie waggled her fingers, but the others went back to what-ever they were talking about, as if I wasn't even there. I noticed all the girls were wearing hip-huggers and poor boys and patterned tights, so at least I was dressed right. As for my hair, if the subject came up, I had a story all ready. I would tell people I had a mysterious ailment that caused a person's hair to go all bumpy and frizzy, but that the effect was only temporary. I had also planned to use the same excuse in case I was asked to dance, saying that the doctor told me to avoid strenuous exercise.

But I could see right off that would not be a problem. Nobody was even talking to me, much less asking me to dance. I looked around for Gretchen, but she was gone. So was the boy named Jake. I stepped past Midge Murphy and saw them, the first couple to brave the empty dance floor. The music had changed to Herman's Hermits and Gretchen and Jake were dancing feverishly to one of their hits, "Henry the Eighth."

"They look cute together, don't they?" Carrie was saying to Julia. "That Gretch can really dance."

"Yeah, she's always been better at physical stuff than me," I put in. "Back in elementary school, she would run the whole six hundred on Field Day. I wasn't about to kill myself for a dumb race, so I just walked it."

Julia and Carrie were staring at me strangely, as if I were a Martian who had blundered into the dance.

"Is that right?" Carrie said, feigning

politeness and poking Julia with her elbow. Both girls were ready to crack up.

"Where did you go to elementary school?" Julia asked, with exaggerated interest.

I knew what was coming; I had heard it before. "Centreville," I muttered.

"*Cen*-treville! Where's *that?*" Carrie screeched. "Is that anywhere near Annandale? It sounds kind of hicky."

"Why don't you ask Gretchen where it is?" I said shortly. "She went there six years, same as I did." Whirling on my heel, I shoved past those snobs and went to find Gretchen.

I hated those girls, with their fancy split-level houses in neat subdivisions, and their fancy station wagons, and their fancy country club pools. I didn't know what Gretchen saw in them. In fact, I even hated Gretchen at that moment. She was supposed to be helping me ease into the in-crowd. Instead, she had deserted me for some guy named Jake, leaving me standing in the middle of the floor like an idiot. If Carrie and Julia were examples of the in-crowd, I wasn't so sure I wanted to join.

I walked over to one of the chairs and sat down. There were lots of other girls sitting along the wall, so I had plenty of company. I noticed with dismay that even though they wore miniskirts and poor boys, they all shared some fatal flaw that kept the boys away as effectively as guard dogs with spiked collars. One girl had buck teeth that could be used for a bottle opener; another girl's hair looked as if she had combed it in a wind tunnel. A feeling of gloom settled over me like a wet blanket. It was always going to be like this. For the rest of my life, I would sit on the sidelines with the rest of the rejects, while the cute, popular girls would be on the dance floor, having all the fun.

The more I watched Gretchen whooping it up with Jake, the more I resented her. She'd lied to me. She'd promised me if I got a new outfit, just like the other girls were wearing, and went to this dance, things would be different. Well, maybe it worked for her, but it wasn't working for me. I wondered what fatal flaw I had, wishing I had never come. I could have been home, drawing. Even going to the dentist was preferable to this agony. I didn't mind my unpopularity half as much as when I was at home, but here the whole world could see nobody liked me.

The girl with the wind-tunnel hair leaned toward me. "It looks like fun, doesn't it?" she yelled over the music.

A song by Paul Revere and the Raiders

was booming. "Personally," I intoned, "I think they all look like jerks out there. All that jumping around. That's not really dancing."

Wind-Tunnel girl leaned closer. "What? I can't hear you!"

I gathered my vocal cords together to repeat what I had said, only louder. "I SAID, THEY ALL LOOK LIKE JERKS OUT THERE!"

Naturally, the song chose that instant to end and everybody on the dance floor heard me. Heads swiveled in my direction. I shrank in my seat and stared at the girl with the wind-tunnel hair, so they would all think *she* had yelled that remark. A few people tittered and Wind-Tunnel blushed a bright red. I felt terrible, but better her than me.

Then Gretchen came over, towing a dark-haired boy with a pained expression, as if he were being dragged to the gallows.

"Kobie, *there* you are!" Gretchen chirped. "I've been hunting you for *ages*. That mob out there is so crushing, I thought you might have gotten squashed!" The dark-haired boy laughed uproariously at her feeble joke. "This is Paul Boggs," Gretchen said. "Paul, this is my best friend, Kobie Roberts."

"Hello," I said dully, expecting him to run the other way.

He smiled weakly, then Gretchen dug him in the ribs and hissed, "Go on — *ask* her!"

"Would you like to dance?" he mumbled. It was quite clear he was only asking me as a favor to Gretchen.

I was about to turn him down, when the music switched to another Herman's Hermits tune. Gretch shrieked, "The Hermit! Come on, you two. Let's see you dance!"

The Hermit was a dance, as well as a song by the same name. I did not know how to do it. Gretchen grabbed my hand and Paul's and hauled us to the middle of the dance floor. Then she found Jake again and started gyrating.

Paul and I stood there a second. All around us kids were lifting up one leg and then one arm, and then changing legs and arms like demented flag-signalers, only without the flags. Paul gave a little shrug, then stuck out one leg and raised his left arm. I tried, I really did, but I could not catch the rhythm. I raised the wrong arm and lifted the wrong leg every time, then I'd stop and watch Paul and try to imitate him, but wound up nearly putting out his eye whenever I raised my arm.

When the dance was finally over, Paul practically ran off the dance floor, his grim duty done, undoubtedly glad he had gotten away before I did further damage. Tears stung my eyes. I couldn't let anybody see me crying, I'd rather die first. I ran through the dispersing crowd, around the stage, and up the steps.

Some boys were sitting on the stage, swinging their feet. I pushed through the velvet curtains, closing them behind me, so I could be alone.

I wasn't alone. Sitting at an upright piano was Stuart Buckley. He looked up from the keyboard in surprise as I came bursting through the curtains.

"Oh, for Pete's sake," I said. "All I need is *you*!"

"What're you griping about?" he returned evenly. "*You're* the one who came back here. Why don't you leave?"

I sat down on the piano bench next to him, which showed how upset I was. "I can't go back out there," I moaned. "I made a complete fool of myself in front of this guy."

Stuart played a few tinkling notes. "Just acting natural, huh? What happened to your hair?"

I ignored that crack. "I might have

known I wouldn't get any sympathy from you."

"What do you expect? You haven't said a word to me at the lockers in weeks. I try to be friendly, but you turn me off."

"*Friendly*!" I cried. "Is your idea of being friendly slamming my locker shut every two seconds and making fun of my drawings? With friends like you, who needs enemies?"

He grinned up at me and if I hadn't hated him so much I would have thought he was kind of cute, in a munchkin sort of way. "Since we're both stuck at this dance, we might as well call a truce. Can you play?"

"The piano?"

"No, the tuba. What do you think?"

I shook my head. "Not a note. I'm not very musical," I said, remembering how uncoordinated I had been on the dance floor.

"I'll teach you to play 'Heart and Soul,'" Stuart offered generously. "Anyone can play that." I let that remark slide while he picked up my fingers and placed them on the white keys in front of me, then demonstrated which keys to push down. "Just keep doing that over and over," he instructed. He picked out a lilting little melody, while I played my same notes over and over.

"Hey!" I said. "I'm playing the piano! This is neat!"

"Let's do it again, so we'll get it right. Then I'll show you how to play my part, okay?" With a flourish, Stuart began playing the melody again. When we had finished, he said, "That was great, Kobie. You'll be ready to give a concert before you know it."

"Really? Do you really think I'm good?" Desperation had driven me to a new low, fishing for compliments from Stuart Buckley. "Can you teach me something else?"

"I think you can handle my part now." He got up to change places with me on the bench, but instead of going *behind* the bench, as a normal person would have done, he crossed in *front* of me, tangling his feet briefly in the pedals. And then, in the cleverest move I had seen outside of the circus, he stumbled and fell across my lap, with his head pressed against my chest.

I sat there, frozen with shock.

"Oh, Kobie," Stuart said, from somewhere beneath my chin. "I'm wild about you. What about you?"

I was wild, all right, but not about him.

The nerve of that little twerp, making a pass at me backstage!

"Get away from me!" I yelled. "Have you lost your mind?"

Stuart sat up then, his glasses crooked, his pale blue eyes puzzled. Things had not gone according to plan for him, either, and he couldn't understand why. Then I did the worst thing I could possibly do. I began to laugh.

Not just a silly little giggle, but a big, guffawing horselaugh. The guffaws dissolved into hysterical laughter. I couldn't stop.

"What are you laughing at?" Stuart demanded. "Are you laughing at *me*?"

I shook my head, unable to speak. The whole situation was so ridiculous.

Stuart flounced away from me, anger and humiliation in every movement of his stubby legs as he stomped off the stage. I stopped laughing, finally, but it was too late. He was gone.

I sat at the piano alone, leaden with the certainty that, because I had scorned Stuart during the height of his fleeting interest in me, he would make my life even more miserable.

Chapter 6

"I don't know what went wrong," Gretchen mused one afternoon, a few weeks after the fateful dance. We were sitting in my bedroom, drinking fruit punch and nibbling pretzels.

"*I* know what went wrong," I said dismally. "I was born, that's what went wrong."

Gretchen leaned against the headboard of my bed. "I thought sure Paul Boggs liked you, Kobie. He asked me to introduce you to him."

"Did he really?" I found that difficult to swallow, recalling the doomed look on his face when Gretchen had dragged him over to me.

"Well, I told him about you *first*," she admitted finally. "I said I had this terrific friend and he said, as terrific as you?"

"And what did *you* say?" Now for the moment of truth.

Gretchen's blue eyes were as round and honest as ever as she replied, "Why, I told him you were lots more fun than me and that's when he asked to meet you."

Today was one of those rare occasions when Gretchen could come over to my house. Her father worked on Saturdays, as mine often did, taking the family car, so there was never any easy way for us to get together. This particular Saturday, Gretchen's father had stayed home, and Gretchen's brother Charles, who had a driver's license, offered to drop Gretchen off at my house on his way to meet his own friends. He had promised to pick her up after supper.

Having Gretchen to myself for one whole day was wonderful. She came over wearing baggy corduroy pants and a striped shirt like I had on, and it was like old times. We goofed around, listening to the radio and talking. I forgot about Gretchen's stockings and genuine madras outfits and the fact she was part of the in-crowd at school, while I was still a nobody. It was only after lunch that the subject of boys and the dance came up.

Right after the dance, when Gretchen

had called to ask if I'd had a good time, I hadn't been sure I ever wanted to speak to her again. I had told her it was okay and wouldn't say any more about it. As the weeks went by, my anger at her had melted by degrees, like a snowman in the sun, and today I confessed the whole sordid affair, how Paul had left me on the dance floor and how I had gone backstage where Stuart Buckley had made a pass at me.

"You put Paul Boggs up to asking me to dance, didn't you?" I asked her now.

Gretchen twirled a piece of hair. She had started wearing it parted in the middle, falling to her shoulders where the ends curved under, like Midge's. "Well, I *did* kind of ask him," she said slowly. "But only because I knew he was too shy to think of it by himself. Some boys need a little push."

"Stuart Buckley doesn't," I said. "I hardly sat down before he was all over me." That was an exaggeration, but I didn't want Gretchen to think I was *too* hopeless.

"Sometimes you have to watch out for the short ones. They have sneaky ways," Gretchen warned.

I poured the last of the fruit punch into our glasses. "I've been thinking about Stuart. . . . He does such terrible things to me, like slamming my locker. Last week he slammed it on my foot. I could hardly slug him, it hurt so much. And he's always nosing around my stuff, pulling out my papers and making a mess."

"If I were you," Gretchen put in, "I'd have gotten my locker changed ages ago. I don't know how you stand it."

"I'm getting used to it. Mom says we all have our burdens to bear in life and I guess Stuart's mine." His horrid behavior *had* gotten worse, just as I had predicted. But amazingly enough, I had grown used to his fiendish little self next to my locker, the way some people learn to tolerate an incurable disease.

"Anyway," I went on, "Stuart reminds me of Nelson Holloway. Do you remember him?"

"Wasn't he that nerdy kid who transferred into our third-grade class halfway through the year? He was the laughing stock of Centreville because he wore a suit coat with shorts."

I nodded. "That's the one. Nelson claimed everybody dressed like that in the boarding school he went to before he came to our school. He used to push me off the merry-go-round at recess, remember? One time he pushed me in a mud puddle and ruined my dress. When the playground teacher took me into the girls' room to clean up, she said Nelson had a crush on me and that's why he acted so awful. She said sometimes boys do that."

Gretchen's face brightened as she saw what I was leading up to. "Boys *do* act really mean around girls they like. Jeff Nichols pulled my braids every single day in the fourth grade, until I hit him, and then he gave me a ring he got in a box of Cracker Jacks." Then she frowned. "So you think Stuart drives you crazy because he likes you."

"Yeah," I answered confidently. "You have to take into account Stuart's feeble little mind. Not only does he *look* like a third grader, but he still *acts* like one." Gretchen was shaking her head. "You don't agree. What do you know that I don't?" I asked.

She sighed. "I hate to break your heart, Kobie, but Stuart is in Drama Club with me. He acts like that around *all* the girls, even me. Nobody can stand him, he's such a pest. We're always plotting ways to get rid of him. Last week Jake said we ought to call the city and have him taken out with the trash. Stuart got so mad, his face turned purple and he called Jake something he shouldn't have in front of the drama teacher. Mr. Fernandez threw him out. I felt sorry for Stuart, but he brought it all on himself."

I hugged my pillow to my chest, hiding my face momentarily from Gretchen. I couldn't even have Stuart Buckley to myself, it seemed. I know Gretchen didn't mean to burst my little bubble that at least *one* boy at Frost liked me, even one as horrible as Stuart. "Oh, well," I said. "It was just a theory."

"Don't lose any sleep over a creep like Stuart," she said. "There are plenty of other boys in school. I bet a boy you know is thinking about you right this very minute, wondering how he's ever going to get your attention."

"That shouldn't be too hard," I said ruefully. "All he has to do is stand still. I'll know he's interested when he doesn't run the other way."

"Speaking of running, did you know Midge Murphy has twenty-three Froot Loops in her wallet?"

I didn't know and I didn't really care if I never heard Midge Murphy's name again as long as I lived. Collecting Froot Loops was the latest craze to hit Frost. All the boys wore Oxford cloth shirts that had a sort of pleat in the back with a fabric loop, supposedly used to hang up the shirt.

The girls chased after the boys like lunatics, ripping the loops off, and sometimes tearing the guy's shirt in the process. Flashing your collection of Froot Loops was a status thing, much the way cavemen displayed pelts in the old days to prove they were great hunters. Froot Loop snatching had gotten so bad, the boys kept their jackets on all day and their mothers called the school, complaining their kids' clothes were being ruined. So now Mr. Gamble, the bald-headed vice-principal, patrolled the halls, determined to keep the girls away from the boys. It did not surprise me that Midge Murphy had so many Froot Loops.

"Do you have any?" I asked Gretchen. I had tried to yank Stuart's loop one day when the little varmint had had his back turned, but instead of giving the loop a quick, twisting jerk, I had pulled and tugged, nearly strangling Stuart. It had been a wonderful feeling.

Gretchen reached beside the bed and pulled her wallet from her purse. Between my last year's school picture and a four-leaf clover she had pasted three Froot Loops — a pale yellow one, a blue striped one, and a burgundy one.

"You pulled loops off *three* guys?" I

couldn't believe she would ever do anything so aggressive. It wasn't her nature.

She shook her head. "Are you kidding? With Gamble running around? I asked Jake for the loops off his shirts and he cut them off for me. They're all Jake's." The implication of her last words was very clear — Gretchen and Jake were an item. If a girl carried the Froot Loops of just one guy, they were going together.

Before I could ask Gretchen if what I was thinking was true, my mother chose that moment to barge into my room, ostensibly to pick up the dirty glasses and empty pretzel bowl, but really to spy on us.

"Kobie, this room is a sight," she declared, her sharp eyes taking in the place. I don't know what she expected to find us doing. Smoking cigarettes? Playing poker? Lately, my mother had gotten awfully suspicious whenever I spent too much time in my room.

"When are you going to clean it up?" she asked. "Or do I have to tell the health department to condemn it?"

"Very funny," I said icily. "What do you *want*, Mom?"

"I bet Gretchen's room isn't as bad as yours," she said. "And I bet Gretchen isn't as rude as you are, either, missy. Let's watch that mouth."

I handed my mother the glasses and bowl, giving her a look that said I thought she had overstayed her welcome. "Gretchen's every bit as bad as I am. Just this morning her mother threatened to send her to prison, isn't that right, Gretch?"

"You're very smart, Kobie," my mother said with undisguised sarcasm. "You think it's cute to talk back to your mother in front of your friends." She stalked out of the room, closing the door behind her as if she wished it were the door to my jail cell.

"Honestly, is your mother as cranky as mine?" I asked Gretchen.

"Worse. She criticizes every little thing I do. She's on my back morning, noon, and night. I can't do anything right."

"You'd think they'd never been our age, the way they act. What's wrong with my room? I know exactly what's in each one of those piles. I arranged them that way on purpose. Just because I don't dust and vacuum every two seconds, I'm a slob."

Gretchen stretched out on my bed, which was, of course, unmade. "Mothers are a real pain, all right."

"Mine used to be halfway decent until this summer. Right after I turned thirteen, she turned into an ogre." I inspected my fingernails to see if they had grown any since last night. Yesterday I had decided to stop biting them, so I would have an excuse to buy nail polish like Gretchen's. "You know, this business of being thirteen can be hazardous to a person's health. Why didn't they hand us a booklet about that when we were in sixth grade, instead of showing us that stupid movie? Let us know what was in store for us."

"Isn't that the truth?" Gretchen agreed. "Remember? We had to have signed permission slips and everything before we could see that movie and it was the biggest farce."

She was right, as usual. All the sixth-grade girls who had gotten their permission slips signed by their parents had been required to attend this special movie. I remember walking past Martin Johnson's desk, puffed up with self-importance. Most of the boys had jeered at us as we filed out, but Martin and a few others had looked at us kind of strangely, as if we would be different when we came back.

The movie had been incredibly dumb. It was supposed to be about "growing into womanhood" and how wonderful life was going to be, once our bodies were finished making us into *women*. I hadn't paid too much attention to that stuff; I was more interested in the animated girl who flitted through the whole thing in a pink swirly dress, looked at herself in the mirror a lot, and radiated pink sparkly dust like Tinker Bell every time her body made a new change. The movie had been very pretty but it hadn't *told* us anything, really, only hinted at these mysterious changes. Whatever was going to happen, it hadn't sounded like much fun.

When the movie was over, we had gone back to class where the boys were busy drawing airplanes and pretending to be nonchalant. Martin Johnson asked me if the movie was about "girls' stuff," and I told him yes, but that he hadn't missed anything.

Gretchen suddenly sat up, interrupting my daydream. She pointed to a flat object lying under my dresser. "What's that?"

I reached over and pulled my record album into view. "I bought this about a month ago. It's got 'Mr. Tambourine Man' and a bunch of other neat songs."

"But the wrapper is still on it," she said, puzzled.

"I didn't want the record to get all scratched."

Gretchen knew I didn't have a record player but she didn't make a big deal of it. "Why don't you come over to my house and you can play it there?"

"Really? That'd be neat. When can I

come over?" I asked eagerly. My favorite song had moved off the Top 40 and wasn't being played over the radio, so I hadn't heard it in ages.

She thought a minute. "How about the Saturday after Thanksgiving? I think my father has off then. Charles can bring you over. We'll have a blast. We can yak and try on makeup."

"Did you bring any with you today?" I asked.

She fished around in her purse and came up with a fistful of Yardley cosmetics: an eye shadow stick, powder, blush-on, Slicker eyeliner, and *four* different lipsticks.

"Wow! Did your mother let you buy all that? Are you ever lucky!" Her mother might be on Gretchen's back morning, noon, and night, but she let Gretchen have anything she wanted.

Gretchen slid off the bed, taking the cosmetics over to my dresser. "I'll do your face, then you do mine."

We spent the next hour making up each other's faces. Gretchen put the stuff on me a lot better than I did her, but she was a good sport about it, even if I did smear the eyeliner on too thick. I tried on all her lipsticks — pale blue, ivory, pale pink, and pale peach. Those pale, nearly white, colors made my mouth look as if it had been erased or, at best, as if I'd been oxygen-deprived for several minutes. But it was the latest fashion and who was I to question it?

As I stared at myself in the mirror over my dresser, I said, "You look better wearing this stuff than I do."

"I do not. You look terrific, Kobie. Real sophisticated. I bet you could pass for eighteen, maybe nineteen."

I thought I looked more like a leftover from Halloween. My features seemed too unformed, like a Polaroid snapshot that wasn't finished developing. Gretchen, on the other hand, had cheekbones and full lips. *She* could pass for eighteen. We pouted in the mirror, trying to be elegant and sophisticated. Then I stuck out my tongue and Gretchen cracked up.

We were still laughing like a couple of crazies when we went into the bathroom to wash our faces.

Chapter 7

The day after Thanksgiving, a drizzly Friday, I stood in the middle of my bedroom, trying to decide what to do first. At breakfast, my mother ordered me to clean my room before I thought about going anywhere the next day, much less to Gretchen's. From the tone in her voice, she sounded as though she planned to have me deported if I didn't hop to it this time.

"*Today*! Not next week or later this weekend. *Today*, do you understand?" she yelled, as I swallowed the excuse forming in the back of my throat.

Besides cleaning my room, I had to do my figure-developing exercises and answer a chain letter — a real stellar line-up. Since I wasn't exactly brimming with enthusiasm at the prospect of shoveling out my hogpen room or ready to deal with the sticky issue of the chain letter, I decided to get my figure-developing exercises out of the way first. With my figure, there wasn't a second to lose.

Gretchen had unearthed an instruction book and given it to me on the bus a couple of weeks ago.

"*One Month to a Charming New You* by Miss Diana?" I read doubtfully as she handed the book to me. "Where did you dig this up?"

"I found it in my mother's bottom drawer when I was hunting for a pair of stockings. I ran my only pair yesterday," she told me. Heaven forbid she should have to come to school wearing babyish old knee socks. "Turn to page 46."

I opened the book and stared at two pages of diagrams, showing drawings of a woman in strange poses. I couldn't tell if she was learning how to fly or practicing to be a contortionist. "What *is* this?"

"Can't you read, dummy? Right there where it says 'How to improve your measurements.' You do those exercises faithfully for one month and I'll bet you get a few curves."

"In my case, a few curves would be a mere drop in the bucket," I said wryly.

"So you do them two months. Or three. The point is, you can take action to improve your figure, Kobie. You're always moaning about how self-conscious you feel in gym. Now you can *do* something about it."

"Okay," I said doubtfully. "I'll give it a try."

I took the book home. That night, in addition to studying the diagrams, I read about the importance of regular depilatories, weight-gain menus that recommended eating peanut butter, cashew, and banana sandwiches washed down with milkshakes six times a day, and the hairstyle that would most flatter my particular face shape. I only had peach-fuzz on my legs, so I could forget about giving myself a depilatory; the diet sounded pretty good but would undoubtedly send our grocery bill through the roof; and the hairdo that most flattered my face shape (long, with a high forehead and at least a yard of chin) had been out of style since World War II.

Now, while rain slithered down the storm windows, I sat down on the floor with my back braced against the edge of my opened closet door, held my arms in a chicken-wing position, and began exercising. Miss Diana's book was beside me, so I could refer to the diagrams every now and then. I had been doing the exercises for two weeks and had yet to see the "stunning results" Miss Diana claimed anybody following her advice would get. Still, maybe there was something to this charm business after all. I vowed to be more charming from that moment on.

When I had finished fifteen sets of each of the five exercises and my rib cage felt dislocated, I put the book away (well, threw it under the bed, actually) and got out the chain letter. I wished Miss Diana had a quick and easy solution for that little problem.

It was my own fault, really. If I hadn't been so eager to take the note Julia Neal had handed me in English class, I wouldn't be stuck with the letter. I had thought Julia was passing me a fun, now-you're-one-of-us type of note, asking me to a slumber party or something. When I had opened it after class and found it was a *chain letter*, she wouldn't take it back.

"It's yours," she said airily. "Possession is nine-tenths of the law."

That might be true but what Julia didn't know was that the *other* tenth decreed that chain letters could be crammed down the giver's throat. But she had already disappeared down the hall, leaving me foolishly holding the thing.

I unfolded the letter now, scanning Julia's rounded, back-slant handwriting.

The letter stated the usual nonsense, about how the chain was started in 1952 in Tibet and how it had been around the world 1,427 times without a single break. I was instructed to copy the letter twenty times, adding my address to the bottom of the list, send a dollar to the address just above mine, then pass (or foist, to be more accurate) copies of the letter on to twenty friends.

The letter certainly took a lot for granted. I didn't have *two* friends, much less twenty, and even if I did, they'd be ex-friends as fast as they learned they'd have to copy the letter twenty times and cough up a dollar.

In two short weeks, I would be rewarded with twenty crisp new dollar bills and also have the luck of the chain. If I broke the chain, *under any circumstances*, there was no telling what awful things would happen to me. Did I want to take that chance? the letter concluded.

I stuffed the letter back in its envelope. "Yes, I do. I'm not answering any dumb chain letter." I tossed the envelope in my trash can with the carefree abandon of someone who has decided to jump from the plane anyway, even though the parachute cord didn't work.

My mother stuck her head in my door just then. "What's going on in here? I don't see any cleaning."

"How come you never knock? Don't you have any respect for a person's privacy?" I growled, instantly reverting back to my normal, uncharming self.

"You haven't *touched* this room, Kobie. I'm not kidding. You are not going to Gretchen's tomorrow if this place isn't spotless."

I picked up the bedcovers trailing from my bed and yanked them up over the sheets. "I said I'd clean it and I will. What's for lunch?"

"You just had breakfast."

"I'm hungry already. What are we having?"

"Turkey sandwiches. And that's not the way to make a bed. Were you brought up in a barn?"

"You ought to know," I wanted to return, but instead I said, "Turkey again? That's all we ever have. Turkey, turkey, turkey."

"We only had it *yesterday* for Thanksgiving dinner. Do you expect me to throw out the leftovers just because you're tired of them?"

"I'd rather have a peanut butter, cashew, and banana sandwich and a milkshake," I said. "It's better for me than dry old turkey."

"We're having turkey and that's final," my mother snapped. "When I come back in one hour, I'd better see some progress on this room."

I hardly knew where to begin, the place was so filthy. But I desperately wanted to go to Gretchen's tomorrow. Gretchen's mother was making a chocolate cake with seven-minute frosting and beans and franks. She didn't make *her* daughter eat turkey for weeks on end. Gretchen had asked me to help her rehearse for the try-outs of *Oliver!*, the show the Drama Club was putting on in the spring. She had also gotten some new makeup, which we would experiment with. But, most of all, I was anxious to play my Byrds album on her record player. After I'd heard "Mr. Tambourine Man" ten or twelve times, the song that had sort of become my private anthem, I knew I'd feel better.

I tackled the nest of clothes in the corner between my dresser and the wall. My good outfits (a total of one and a half) I always hung up in my closet immediately after school, but the rest of my clothes I tossed in the corner. It was much more convenient than fooling with hangers — I'd take a top and a pair of slacks from the pile, wear

97

them, then throw them back on the pile when I was done. Very handy. Naturally, my mother objected violently to this system and flatly refused to wash or iron anything in the pile, until I put them in the hamper where they belonged.

I lifted my brown corduroy pants from the top of the pile and sniffed. Maybe these things *could* stand to be washed. I brought the hamper in from the bathroom and began shoving clothes into it. When laundry day rolled around, my mother was going to be thrilled. I came across the Ugliest Dress in the World, wrinkled and moldy-smelling. I put it in the hamper even though it really deserved a burial at sea. While I pulled out seemingly hundreds of dresses and tops, I hummed a little. The rain pattered down the windowpanes and the faint wail of an ambulance whined up the road. Cleaning my room on a rainy day wasn't so bad, after all. It was actually kind of pleasant to be working, but I wouldn't dare let on to my mother.

At the bottom of the pile I found my cutoffs and yellow cropped top. The last time I had worn that outfit was at the beach with Gretchen. It *had* been a while since I went through the pile. When I lifted the last piece, an enormous spider skittered under my dresser. I was fascinated and horrified. Imagine sharing quarters with an insect that huge and not knowing about its existence!

I was sifting through old school papers that had somehow accumulated under my bed when the phone rang. Glancing at my bedside clock, I realized it was too early for Gretchen to call, so I let my mother answer it. The phone was in my parent's room across the hall. I could hear her muffled voice, sounding at first inquiring and then very serious.

"I'll go tell her right now," my mother said and then hung up. The call obviously concerned me; I was the only other "her" in the house besides my mother.

I was halfway to the door when she came in. "Tell me what?" I demanded. "Who was that on the phone?"

Her face was grim. "It was Gretchen's father. Gretchen and her brother were in an accident about an hour ago."

My heart stopped. "What? Is she all right?"

My mother took my arm and guided me over to my lumpy bed. "She's alive, Kobie. But she's been hurt."

"How? Where is she hurt? Is she in the hospital?" The questions came tumbling from my lips. I wasn't getting answers fast enough. "Tell me what happened!"

"Charles and Gretchen were on their way to the store. The road was wet and he lost control of the car making the turn across Lee Highway. He crashed into a tree. No other cars were involved. Charles hit the steering wheel. He was knocked out for a few minutes. Gretchen's father said he lost a lot of teeth but that was about all. Neither of them were wearing seat belts."

"What about Gretchen?"

My mother paused, as if searching for the right way to break it to me. "Gretchen was hurt worse than her brother. Her head went through the windshield. Her father says she has a deep gash near her eye. The ambulance we heard a while ago was for them — they were taken to Fairfax Hospital. That's where Mr. Farris called me from. Gretchen is in surgery right now. That's all he could tell me."

I tried to take it all in. It wasn't possible! How could I be cleaning my room while Gretchen was having a terrible accident? I'd even heard the siren of the ambulance going up the highway and never thought a thing about it, and the whole time, Gretchen was inside, bleeding.

"Can we go to the hospital?" I asked.

"Honey, it won't do any good. Her family is there. Her father promised to call the minute he heard any news. Anyway, you won't be able to see her. No children under sixteen are allowed past the lobby. That's a hospital rule."

"I'm not a child!" I cried, hating the feeling of helplessness that suddenly came over me. "Gretchen is my best friend. She needs me!"

"Right now, she needs her family with her," my mother said gently. "She'll be all right, Kobie. And we'll go see her as soon as she's home from the hospital."

"When will that be?" I asked, thinking about the day we were going to spend together — tomorrow! Why did this have to happen on today of all days? Why did it have to happen at all?

"I don't know. Soon." My mother ruffled my hair. "Come on. We can't wait for news on an empty stomach. Let's go fix lunch. I'll bet we hear before we finish eating."

Gretchen's father didn't call until after supper that evening. I was nearly out of my mind. My mother talked to him, promising to relay exactly what he said to me. Gretchen's surgery had lasted longer than they thought it would, but she was in fair condition, considering she had lost so much blood. No, I couldn't call her in her room at the hospital, she was heavily sedated. But she should be better in a day or so and we could talk then.

Since our house was on the way to the hospital, Gretchen's father said he would stop by and pick up the fruit basket my mother planned to get the next day.

"Why don't you make Gretchen a get well card?" she suggested. "Something funny to cheer her up."

For once I didn't balk and moan as I usually did over any suggestion my mother made. I got out my crayons and paper and inks and began copying a picture from one of my comic books, a panel where Donald Duck is bandaged and limping after being thrown from a horse.

"Hope you're back in the saddle again real soon!" I lettered on the front of the card. Inside I wrote, "Dear Gretchen, I'm sorry you were in a car wreck. I bet it was terrible. I'll tell Julia and Midge about it Monday at lunch. And I'll go around to your teachers and get your homework assignments so you won't get too far behind. Mom says you'll probably be back at school in a few weeks. I hope so. I miss you. Love, Kobie."

I put the finishing touches on the card, then looked around for an envelope to put it in. There was the envelope that chain letter had come in — but my waste basket was empty. My mother had taken pity on me and finished cleaning my room herself. She had emptied the trash and vacuumed the rug.

I glanced out the window, a feeling of dread creeping over me. It had stopped raining and my father was in the far corner of the yard, dumping garbage into the trash burner. A wisp of smoke curled upward; he had already started the fire. Too late to get the letter back now.

Suddenly I knew why Gretchen had been in the accident. It was because I had broken the chain.

Chapter 8

Gretchen was in the hospital a lot longer than I expected. She had to have another operation, this time to remove a fragment of glass from her eye. The deep cut was healing well, according to the reports Gretchen's father gave us when he stopped at our house to pick up the cards and little presents from me, but the doctors were concerned about her vision and some other things and were keeping her there for observation.

Life was unbearably lonely without Gretchen, especially since she wouldn't talk to me on the phone. I called the hospital every day after school but Gretchen's roommate always answered and said that Gretchen was sleeping or out of the room at the moment. And Gretchen never called me back. It was as if she had amnesia and had forgotten we were best friends.

When I asked Gretchen's father why she refused to talk on the phone, he shook his head and said she was having a rough time. He hoped I would come to see his daughter after she got home, to cheer her up. I was dying to see her, but until she was released from the hospital, I simply had to wait.

At school, things dragged along with agonizing slowness. In phys. ed., we finally finished field hockey and began an indoor unit on health, which gave my bruised legs a break until we began the next sport. My shirtwaist dress was mostly done — I was two weeks behind because I had put the sleeves in upside down and the collar on backward. Mrs. Vandenheuvel still passed around "Peanuts" each morning before delivering the day's rapid-fire history lecture. Just after Thanksgiving, we got back our notebooks, graded. She gave me a "C +", a very generous mark considering half my notes were blank. I had forgotten to fill in the shorthand symbols.

I missed Gretchen terribly. Not just on the bus to and from school, but especially at lunch. Midge and Julia let it be known they had only tolerated my presence because of Gretchen. Now that Gretchen was out sick, they moved to another table, leaving me to sit alone.

And then Stuart Buckley changed lunch

shifts, causing my life to take a swift downward spiral.

Previously, the one bright spot of my school day was lunchtime, not only because of Gretchen, but because Stuart had the "B" shift, which meant I didn't have to look at his weasely face a whole blissful half hour.

Gretchen had been in the hospital about two weeks and I was at my empty table, removing the paper wrapper from my straw and minding my own business, when something small but very powerful hurtled itself across the room to crash into the chair across from me and send my plate flying into my lap. I jumped up quickly, but not before meat loaf and mashed potatoes slithered down my leg.

"Safe!" cried a familiar voice. "Boy, Kobie, what a slob you are!"

I looked up from my potato-globbed skirt to see Stuart Buckley grinning at me. "Darn it, Stuart!" I yelled. "I have to go around the rest of the day like this! Why were you ever put on this planet?"

"Just to torment you," he replied with an angelic smile.

"I believe it. What are you doing here? You don't eat lunch this shift."

"I do now. Isn't that great? I came in the door and the first person I saw was you,

Kobie, sitting all alone and forlorn-looking. And now I'm here to eat lunch with you, every day till school is out. Aren't you excited?"

"Thrilled," I said dryly. "Just what I need — terminal indigestion. How come you decided to plague me now?"

"I got thrown out of my regular shift," he said, sampling the cherry cobbler from my tray. "You don't want this, do you?"

"Not now I don't. How can you get thrown out of *lunch*?"

He shrugged. "The lunch monitor told the principal I was too disruptive. I have no idea what she was talking about. Anyway, they moved me here. Maybe they thought it was better if I ate earlier."

I doubted it. If I'd had the misfortune to have Stuart in one of my classes or lunch shifts, I would have done anything to get him transferred, too.

Stuart descended on my table like a tornado every day about twelve seconds after I got my tray. He never bought lunch or brought anything from home, preferring to beg from me. He would point to my dessert or roll, poking his finger right down in the food, and then ask me if I wanted it, as if I could eat anything his grubby hands had mauled. When I asked him why he didn't buy his *own* lunch, he merely shrugged and said nothing looked good to him that day. Apparently, the grass was greener on my side of the table, because he always managed to find three or four things that looked good to him, as long as they came from my tray.

I couldn't figure out that kid. He still drove me insane by slamming my locker. One day he closed it on my little finger. When he saw my hand trapped in the door, he actually turned pale and opened the locker again, double-quick. My finger was only mangled temporarily, but Stuart was very concerned and made me go to the nurse's office. The next day, however, when he saw I was going to live, he went back to slamming my locker.

I often thought Stuart would be a great weapon against an enemy's army.

"Come in, Kobie." Gretchen's mother greeted me at the door with a tired smile. "It's nice to see you again. Cold today, isn't it? Have you finished your shopping yet? Christmas is next week, you know."

"I haven't even started," I confessed, putting my coat on the chair.

"Gretchen is in her room. You can go on back."

"Thanks," I told her, and went through

the living room to the back of the house where the bedrooms were located.

Gretchen's door was closed. I braced myself, then knocked.

"Come in," Gretchen said.

I opened the door gingerly, as if expecting some wild animal to lunge at me from the other side. I hadn't talked to or seen Gretchen since the accident. Even though she had been home from the hospital a whole week, it was her mother who had invited me over today.

Gretchen was lying on her bed, paging through *Tiger Beat* magazine. She sat up as I came in and the first thing I noticed was that she wore glasses, heavy, black-framed glasses like a librarian would wear. She had her hair fixed a new way, too, with soft curls around her temples.

"Hi Gretch." I closed the door behind me softly. "How're you feeling?"

"Okay." She made no move to get off the bed. I wanted to give her a big hug, but her blue eyes, cold behind the new glasses, told me to keep my distance.

"Here are some comics." I set the pile down on her dresser. I had almost brought my Byrds album, but I hadn't wanted Gretchen to get the wrong idea, thinking I had only come to play my record instead of to see her. "I would've brought your homework assignments, but your home-room teacher said you're getting a tutor. Is that true?"

"Yeah. A lady from the County is going to help me catch up through the holidays, and then I'll see about going back to Frost." She went back to her magazine.

I couldn't believe this was the same Gretchen. She acted like I was the census-taker or something. Why was she ignoring me? "Gretch, how come you didn't want to talk to me when you were in the hospital?"

"I didn't talk to anybody, not just you."

"But why? I was dying to find out how you were."

She didn't answer, but reached over to her nightstand to get a pack of gum. After cramming a stick in her own mouth, she offered the pack to me. "Want some?"

I moved closer to take the gum. As I did, I could see the red, raw-looking scar that ran from her hairline down her temple to the corner of her right eye. It wasn't grue-some like Frankenstein's railroad-track scar or anything, but it was still a shock to see her pretty face marked that way.

She caught me staring and brushed her hair over the side of her face. "It's gross, isn't it?"

I sat down on the bed. "Not really. In fact, it — isn't as bad as I expected. Do you have to wear glasses now?"

She nodded. "I can't see as good as I did before the accident. The doctor told me I'd probably have to wear them the rest of my life. I hate these frames, but see this extra-thick part?" She pointed to the earpiece over her temple. "It helps hide the scar and that's supposed to make me less self-conscious, the doctor said."

"Does it work?"

She looked at me, then away again. "No," she said in a small voice. "I feel like everybody's staring at me."

I didn't know what to say. "Did you like the cards I sent?"

She managed a smile. "I loved them. I've kept every one. They're in my nightstand, along with a lot of other stuff people sent me. I even got a card from Jake. Want to see?" She got up to rummage through the bottom drawer, then handed me a card decorated with hearts and birds.

"It looks like a valentine," I said. "Can I read what he wrote?"

"Sure."

Under the gooey get-well verse, Jake had written, "I hope you get better for the next dance. Miss you, love, Jake." He had filled the remaining white space with "x's" and "o's," meaning hugs and kisses.

"He really likes you," I said, giving the card back to her. "You're so lucky to have a guy like Jake."

"Well, actually, I have *two* guys," she said, rather triumphantly.

"Two? Who's the second one?"

"His name is David. He was the boy who found us right after the accident. David's father was in the car behind us when we hit the tree. He stopped and ran to a house to call for help. David stayed with me."

"I thought you were knocked out," I said.

"I was, but only for a minute. I remember almost everything that happened. I remember when the back wheels of our car sort of spun around and I remember Charles trying to grab me, but it was too late. I don't remember hitting the tree, but I remember this kind voice saying, 'Take it easy. Help is on the way.' That was David. He pulled me out of the car and put me in their car and held me in his arms until the ambulance came."

I sat with my mouth hanging open. This was like a movie — I had never heard anything so romantic.

"He even rode in the ambulance with me. He never left my side. While the paramedic tried to stop my face from bleeding, David sat by the stretcher, holding my hand the whole time. I remember saying, 'I've gotten your shirt all bloody!' but he just smiled and told me not to worry about it. David and his father stayed with my parents until I was out of surgery. And David came to see me three times while I was in the hospital.''

I recalled the no-children-under-sixteen rule that had prevented me from going to see her. "How old is this guy?"

"Seventeen. Kobie, he's so cute. You can't imagine how cute he is. Blond hair, blue eyes." Her voice went all dreamy just picturing him.

"Gosh, Gretchen. Only *you* could have a terrible accident and get some cute guy." I was trying to be funny, but Gretchen got all huffy.

"I was almost *killed*, Kobie," she said, but then her face crumpled a bit as if she realized the price she was paying to be able to say that wasn't worth a few seconds of glory.

"I know," I said. "I missed you at school. It's been awful."

"Well, I wasn't exactly having a picnic, myself. I had two operations and they both hurt like crazy. I had twenty-two stitches. And it's not over yet. My doctor says I have to have at least one more operation to fix my scar."

"What do you mean, fix it?" I asked hesitantly.

"Plastic surgery," Gretchen intoned.

"You mean like a movie star? You're getting a face-lift?"

She sighed, exasperated. "Do I *look* like I need a face-lift? For Pete's sake, Kobie, I wish you'd grow up. They're going to do a skin graft. Take a little piece of skin from some other part of my body and sew it over my scar, so it'll look more normal."

All this talk of stitches and sewing made me feel queasy. I couldn't even stand to have my mother dig a splinter out of my finger, much less imagine what Gretchen had been through. "I hope your doctor is a better sewer than I am. Did I tell you I put the sleeves of my dress in upside-down? And the collar on backwards? Mrs. Humphrey said she's never seen such a mess in all her forty-eight years of teaching."

"I don't think that's very funny, Kobie. Do you know what it's like to have somebody sewing your skin? It's the absolute worst torture in the world." She flung herself back against her pillows, ripping off her new, hateful glasses and turning her face away from me again.

I almost said that the absolute worst torture in the world was having to eat lunch with Stuart Buckley, but thought better of it. I was supposed to be cheering Gretchen up, but instead I seemed to be making her feel bad, reminding her of her operations and all.

I glanced around her room. "Did you get some new curtains? I don't remember seeing those before."

Her voice muffled, Gretchen replied, "Mom bought new curtains and this bedspread before I came home from the hospital. I guess she thought new stuff would make up for having an ugly face. It doesn't, though. Nothing does."

I hated to hear Gretchen talk this way. She had always been the one to look on the bright side of things. Then I noticed the mirror over her dresser had been removed. A poster of two puppies and a kitten hung in its place. The hand mirror on her nightstand was gone, too. And the new curtains had been pulled tight across the single window.

Gretchen's room looked closed off, as if she was trying to wall herself away from the rest of the world. Something about the missing mirrors jogged a long-forgotten memory to the surface. The penny arcade at Ocean City on the last night of our vacation . . . the tang of salt in the air and my horrible nausea brought on by too much boardwalk junk food . . . Madame Zaza, the mechanical gypsy fortune-teller, and her predictions. "A room without mirrors is like a body without a soul." That had been mine. At the time the fortune hadn't made a bit of sense, but now it seemed to have come true.

And then there was Gretchen's fortune, the one she'd tried to throw away immediately after reading. What was it? Something about dark days ahead. Well, they were certainly here.

I thought about how wonderful Gretchen's life had been going before the accident: She had had more friends than she could count, terrific clothes, a guy who was crazy about her, a mother who let her have whatever she wanted. . . . Now, looking at the rumpled figure lying on the bed, none of that seemed very important.

Something puzzled me. If any of that fortune-telling nonsense could be believed, and I could build a pretty strong case for it from what I saw before me, why did both our fortunes, Gretchen's *and* mine, come true for *her?* I was the one who had broken the chain letter. Why did this terrible thing happen to Gretchen? Most of all, where did that leave me?

Chapter 9

On a cold January morning, I dashed from the bus into the school and down the hall to Gretchen's locker, which was located in the math and science wing. Julia Neal and Midge Murphy were there, waiting for me.

"About time," Midge said.

"I couldn't make the bus go any faster," I retorted. "Anyway, Gretchen isn't here yet." I pulled the cardboard WELCOME BACK sign from between my books and handed it to Julia, while I dug the roll of Scotch tape out of my coat pocket.

Julia held the sign out admiringly. "Gosh, Kobie, this is great. Isn't it great, Midge? You draw better than anybody I know." In her enthusiasm over the poster, Julia forgot for a moment that she was talking to me. She helped me stick the poster on the front of Gretchen's locker, right under the loops of crepe paper she and Midge had already tacked up. A bunch of balloons was tied to the locker handle.

Midge looked critically at my drawing of Sleeping Beauty's castle from Disneyland, with the familiar Disney characters waving out front. "You should be on the committee to make posters for *Oliver!*" she said, giving me a back-handed compliment.

I removed a corner of the tape to straighten the poster. "Mmmmm," I replied absently, wanting them to think I had better things to do than make posters for their dumb old spring show.

Gretchen was coming back to school that day for the first time since her accident, and I felt plumped up with importance. After all, Gretchen was *my* best friend and I had more of a right to be there than anybody. I moved away slightly, to let Midge and Julia know I tolerated their presence, but only just.

The first bell rang and I realized I hadn't been to my own locker yet. I still had on my coat and I hadn't gotten my books for first period.

"Where *is* she?" Julia said. "Why didn't she come on the bus?"

"Her mother said it's too cold for her to stand at the bus stop. A neighbor is driving her in." I craned my neck, straining for a glimpse of Gretchen in the thinning crowds. And then I saw her, making her way hesitantly down the hall. "There she is!" I cried, running to meet her. I wanted Gretchen to see me first, so she would know it was all my idea to have this little welcome-back celebration.

"Surprise!" I cried as she caught sight of me.

Gretchen smiled when she saw me capering in front of her locker, then her smile broadened as she took in the decorations. Julia and Midge were posed on either side of Gretchen's locker, like those girls on game shows who stand glamorously next to refrigerators and washer-dryers.

"Hi, Gretch!" Midge said. "Welcome back!"

"You guys are too much." Gretchen was obviously pleased. "That poster is terrific. Do I get to keep it?"

"Sure. It's yours," I said. The late bell rang. "Oh, darn, I don't have time to go to my own locker."

Gretchen twirled her combination lock. "I can't believe I still remember it, it's been so long. Put your coat in my locker, Kobie. At least you won't have to drag it to class."

I didn't really want to take off my coat in front of Julia and Midge. I shrugged out of the burgundy stadium coat, my "big" Christmas present that year, and hung it on the hook inside Gretchen's locker. Gretchen was looking anxiously at her reflection in the little mirror just inside the door, arranging her curls over her right temple.

"What in the world have you got on?" Julia asked.

"My home ec project," I replied glumly. "We're having a fashion show in class and we have to model our dresses. I think Mrs. Humphrey is really cruel, making us wear them all day in school, where everybody can see us."

Midge and Julia poked each other, smothering laughter, but Gretchen was still fretting over her reflection.

"Oh, it's not too bad, Kobie," she said, barely glancing at my dress.

"That's easy for *you* to say," I argued. "You got excused from your project." The minute I said the words, I bit my tongue.

Gretchen stared at me. "Would you like to trade places with me, Kobie? I'll gladly take the bad grade you're going to get on that dress and you can have all the incompletes I'm going to get on my report card this term."

"Kobie, that was a tactless thing to say." Midge jumped in, linking her arm in Gretchen's. "And on her first day back."

"I'm sorry," I mumbled. "Don't make a federal case out of it, okay?"

"I'll walk you to homeroom," Midge told Gretchen.

"See you at lunch, Kobie." Gretchen left with Julia on one side and Midge on the other, leaving tactless old Kobie to clump off to homeroom by herself.

Nothing was going the way I had planned. *I* was supposed to walk Gretchen to her homeroom. Last night, before I went to sleep, I lay in bed picturing Gretchen's excitement at being back in school with me again. Gretchen's mother had confided to my mother that she thought Gretchen needed to get back into a routine again, that she moped around the house and missed her friends. Midge was right; I shouldn't have said what I did to Gretchen on her first day back after such a long absence. But what about me? Did anybody care that while Gretchen was out, I was left to fend for myself?

In home ec, Mrs. Humphrey told us we would model our dresses in alphabetical order, which meant I was one of the last to walk down the "runway." It also meant I had to sit and watch the other girls parade back and forth in their beautifully made dresses, knowing mine would get the worst grade in the class.

Last Friday I had taken my dress and sewing supplies home and had asked my mother in desperation if she could sort of fix the mistakes. My mother had taken one look at my project and thrown her hands in the air.

"You call this a dress? You just wasted the money we spent on that expensive fabric. *Wasted* it!"

"Please, Mom. Can't you do anything about the cuffs? And the buttonholes? I never could get the hang of buttonholes." I had hung on the back of my mother's sewing chair and whined for ten minutes until she'd given in.

"Go away and leave me alone. I'll see what I can do with this mess." She'd worked all weekend, ripping and basting and ironing. Sunday night she'd unplugged her sewing machine, saying, "This is the best I can do, Kobie. I put the zipper in right and reworked your buttonholes, but there wasn't much I could do about those tucks or the cuffs. If you hadn't ruined all the scrap material, I could have made new ones."

"That's okay." I'd been delirious with joy that she'd been able to salvage as much as she had. I'd blown her a kiss. "Thanks,

Mom. This is the nicest thing you've done for me since you brought me home from the hospital!"

As I'd left the room I'd thought I'd heard her mutter, "Sometimes I wish I'd left you there," but surely a mother wouldn't say a thing like that about her own daughter, would she?

Now, I watched Mrs. Humphrey beam with pride at the students who hadn't given her heartburn by hemming the skirts of their dresses closed, or calling her over to the machine every five seconds because they had broken another needle or gotten their bobbin threads snarled again. Those girls modeled their dresses gracefully, confident every stitch was perfect. Naturally, Mrs. Humphrey gave them all "A's."

The last five or six of us left to model went to the back of the room, where a screen had been set up in front of the three-way mirror, so we could primp and straighten our sleeves just before we pranced down the runway. In the mirror I saw that nothing short of a hurricane could straighten the sleeves of my dress and that the three-way view only confirmed in triplicate that my dress looked terrible from all angles. I decided to limp, pretending I had a blister on one foot, so Mrs.

Humphrey wouldn't notice how crooked the hem was.

For lack of anything better to do while waiting for my turn, I gripped the edges of the two outer mirrors and pulled them inward until I was completely enclosed in a triangle of dark glass. I pivoted within the confined space, making faces at my three images, which appeared shadowed and sinister. My reflections stared back at me with hollow, deep-socketed eyes and a round, black mouth hole. I hardly recognized myself.

"Kobie Roberts!" Mrs. Humphrey called, her voice raw with irritation. "Kobie, where are you?"

I swung the mirrors open with relief and hurried to the front of the class. I walked down the aisle, feeling Mrs. Humphrey's hard, flinty stare on me and concentrated on not tripping.

"C minus," she pronounced, as if she were the governor granting me a pardon. "I hope you do better in cooking."

On my way up to the cafeteria line, I saw that Julia and Midge were already at their special table, with two extra seats reserved. One for Gretchen and one for me. I ran through the line so fast, I nearly forgot my plate.

Stuart was waiting at the table I had been forced to eat at while Gretchen was out sick. He waved to me eagerly and I saw he had laid napkins, little packets of salt and pepper, and straws at each of our places. This was his latest kick — to fix up our table as if we were attending a picnic. He acted almost human, too, and I wondered if he had recently been clobbered with a copy of *Emily Post*.

Today I had no time for Stuart.

"Kobie!" he yelled as I breezed by. "Where are you going?"

"Over there. Gretchen came back to school today. You remember, my friend who was in the accident? I'm sitting with her and some others." I resolutely marched past my old table, the napkins and packets of salt, and Stuart's hurt look. He'll get over it, I thought, setting my tray down across from Julia.

"Where's Gretchen?" I asked her.

"I don't know. We thought she was with you."

"She's not in any of my classes," I said. "I never see her until lunch." I pointed to Midge. "She's in *your* English class — didn't you see her?"

Midge took a swallow of milk. "She sits up front now. On account of her eyes.

When the bell rang, she left in a big rush. I thought she went to meet you."

I didn't like the sound of that. "I'll go down to the nurse's office. Maybe she felt sick or something."

Gretchen was not in the nurse's office or in the library or any other logical place. I was about to give up when I found her in the girls' room next to the cafeteria. The place was deserted, except for Gretchen standing by the sink. A lot of little bottles and jars sat on the edge of the sink. She was crying.

"Here you are, Gretch. I've been all over looking for you. What's the matter?" I went over to her but she turned away.

Her face was splotchy from crying and the scar over her eye stood out redder than ever. "Go away," she sobbed. "I don't want you here."

"Why not? I'm your best friend. What are you doing in here, anyway? Lunch is almost over." I picked up one of the little jars to examine it.

"I'm not hungry. Go back and eat." She snatched the jar away from me and began smearing the flesh-colored liquid over her scar.

"You missed a spot," I said helpfully. "Right there." I daubed some of the liquid on my finger and started to apply it to her face. Gretchen backed away, as if I'd come at her with a branding iron.

"Will you leave me alone? Go *away*, Kobie. Get out!"

"I will not. I have as much right as anybody to be in here. It's a free country. What's the *matter* with you, Gretch? You act like you hate me all of a sudden."

She swiped at spilled makeup with a tissue. "I don't hate you, Kobie. I just wish I hadn't come back. Everybody stares at me like I'm a freak. It's awful."

"I guess they'll stare for a while. But then they'll get used to the way you look and stop."

"But *I* won't get used to the way I look! I hate it every time I look in a mirror."

We both gazed at our reflections in the soap-scummy mirror over the sink. My face looked as bland and dumb as ever, but Gretchen's looked startled, like a cave creature suddenly exposed to sunlight.

"Is it that bad?" I asked.

"Worse. Oh, everybody *seems* nice, but they look at me and then they look away real quick, like they're expecting my eyeball to fall out or something. And everybody keeps asking me about the accident and about my operations. They don't really want to know — it's just morbid curiosity. I can't stand it, Kobie."

"What are you going to do? You have to go to school. It's the law." If it wasn't, I would have dropped out long ago, rather than put up with Stuart Buckley.

She drew in a deep breath. "No, I don't. I mean, I don't have to *come* to school. I can learn at home, with the tutor."

"But I thought the tutor was only to help you catch up." I panicked at the thought of not having Gretchen around for the rest of the year.

"If I can get my doctor to say it's too hard for me at school, then I can stay home." She sounded serious.

"Will your doctor do that?" I asked, worried.

She dabbed fiercely at her covered-over scar with a cotton ball. "I don't care if he doesn't. I'm not coming back here after today, Kobie. Nobody can make me."

I helped her gather up her creams and lotions and put them back in the little zippered case she carried in her purse. "Are you going to finish your classes today?" I asked her.

"I have to. My neighbor isn't coming to pick me up until school is out." With a last, regretful look at herself in the mirror, she said, "You know what hurt the worst, Kobie?" I shook my head. "Jake. He saw me in the hall and he just waved and said hi. That's all. He didn't stop to talk or anything. I kind of thought he'd ask me to the dance Friday. I suppose nobody wants to dance with old Scarface," she said bitterly.

"That may not be it at all," I said. "Maybe Jake forgot about you, you've been out so long. It's a well-known fact boys have the attention span of plants."

"I don't think so." Gretchen opened her wallet and took out Jake's Froot Loops. She went into a stall and flushed the toilet.

I couldn't think of a thing to say to make her feel better. "I just wish — " I began.

She turned and the harsh light fell on her scar, picking out the redness even with makeup slathered over it. "What? What do you wish?" she asked.

"Nothing." Wishing was pointless now — everything had changed.

I thought about all those times Gretchen had been there for me, encouraging me to join clubs, and introducing me to people at the dance, and giving me Miss Diana's charm book so I could improve my measurements. I wished I could draw Gretchen's face back the way it was before the accident, so we could go on being best friends and finish out our eighth-grade year in a blaze of glory, as we'd planned at the beach last summer.

Chapter 10

Mrs. Ryerson was unhappy with my color wheel. Since I didn't want to do the project in the first place, that made two of us.

"This isn't the kind of work I expect from you, Kobie, dear." My art teacher looked terribly disappointed, as if she'd just learned I spent my spare time robbing banks. "Last year your work showed such promise, but this year — "

This year is a whole new ball game, I felt like telling her. Somebody had changed the line-up and the current score was Kobie–zero; the rest of the world was clearly winning.

"Now look at this one by a girl in second period," Mrs. Ryerson was saying, as she pulled a piece of cardboard from beneath the stack on her desk. She held up a Valentine heart made up entirely of bits of ripped paper in shades of red and pink.

"It's not exactly a wheel and it doesn't show all the colors but it's very original. Now yours, Kobie — "

"I know. Mine is crummy," I said. "Do you want to set fire to it?"

"Don't be silly. It could have been a fine color wheel, but your colors are a bit — muddy."

Part of the problem, and by far the biggest, was that I just didn't care about anything anymore, not even art. Gretchen was definitely not coming back to school the rest of the year. Even during those weeks she was out sick, I always knew she'd come back eventually and we'd pick up where we left off before the accident.

It was now February. Winter was just revving up, and though I was heartily sick of it already, there were still many slushy, cold weeks to suffer through before the first peep of spring.

All of this added to my attitude problem, though I really had no excuse for handing in such a shabby art project, especially to someone as nice as Mrs. Ryerson. It wasn't *her* fault I was having such a miserable year.

"Would you like me to do this over?" I offered.

"No. Somehow I don't think you'd do it any better a second time." Mrs. Ryerson sighed. "I hope you're not losing interest in art, Kobie. As I've said many times before, I believe you have great talent."

I thought about the plastic insurance folder of my Disney drawings, still on the top shelf in my locker. At the beginning of the year I had been bursting with enthusiasm about my drawing, eager to share with Mrs. Ryerson the work I had done over the summer and the letter I had received from Walt Disney Studios in Burbank, California. Now it all seemed stupid and futile. The letter from Disney Studios was a brush-off and I hadn't drawn any new pictures in ages, not counting the get-well cards I'd made for Gretchen or the welcome-back poster. The great talent Mrs. Ryerson thought I had must have dried up and blown away.

The next day, I was surprised to find Stuart Buckley sitting at my lunch table.

I hadn't seen him in the cafeteria since the day I'd snubbed him to go sit with Julia and Midge and Gretchen. When Gretchen hadn't returned to school, Julia and Midge had sat with their other friends, leaving me to crawl back to no-man's land. I was so lonesome, I even missed Stuart. Not wanting to advertise my friendless state, I read my history book while I ate, but the life and times of George Washington, dull enough the first time around in class, did not go down any easier accompanied by Salisbury steak.

"Haven't seen you in a while," I said to Stuart as I put my tray down. "Except for the occasional locker slam, that is. Where've you been?"

"What do you care?" He sneezed, then wiped his nose on his shirt sleeve. His eyes were streaming behind his glasses and his nose was red and dripping.

"Bad cold, huh?" I handed him one of my paper napkins.

"Brilliant deduction. Where are all your friends?" he said nastily, and I knew he was still miffed about the other day.

"I don't have any." I pushed my cherry cobbler over to him. He pushed it back. "Aren't you hungry? You're usually ravenous. I thought I'd give it to you now so you wouldn't dribble all over my food."

He put his head in his hands.

"Are you all right?" I asked. "You look sort of feverish."

"I *am* feverish. I have a temperature and I feel awful." His normally adenoidal voice was barely above a whisper, he was so hoarse.

"You shouldn't be in school if you're too sick to hold your head up," I said, propping my history book in front of my tray as a germ shield. "Why don't you go home?"

"I can't."

"Why not?"

"There's nobody home to let me in. My father is at work and so is my stepmother," he explained stonily.

"Well, call her and tell her you're sick and you have to come home," I suggested.

He shook his head. "I can't do that. She wouldn't like it if I bothered her at work."

"But if you're *sick* — "

"I'm well enough to be at school, according to her," he said. "It's her fault I got this cold, making me wait outside till she gets home from work."

"You mean you have to stand outside your own house? Why won't she give you a key?" I asked with genuine shock.

He shrugged, his stock reaction to anything he didn't want to answer. "It'll be warm weather again soon and then I won't mind waiting."

"If you don't die of pneumonia first. Why don't you ask your *father* for a key? You have a right to go in your own house." I was adamant.

"He always takes *her* side," Stuart said. "They just got married and she doesn't like me. I don't care. When school is out,

I can go live with my grandmother. She's trying to get custody, anyway."

I thought about this while chewing my ham and cheese sandwich. Poor Stuart. No wonder he was so obnoxious, with a terrible home life. I decided to be nicer to him and forget about the horrible things he'd done to me in the past. Let bygones be bygones. I was about to offer him the other half of my sandwich when he began kicking my chair under the table.

"Stop it," I said. He kept on. "Will you cut it out? Stop kicking my chair."

He never said a word, just stared blankly at me. His kicks got harder. I tried shifting my chair but that only landed me a kick on the shins. "Stuart, if you don't quit it this second — "

I never got to finish my threat. With the toes of his shoes, Stuart pulled my chair forward so fast, I was suddenly squashed against the edge of the table. Then, when I thought I was going to be cut in half, he pulled again, sending my chair toppling over backward. The next thing I knew I was looking up at the ceiling. My head hurt and I couldn't say a word, the wind had been knocked from me. The thanks I got for feeling sorry for the troll!

Then Stuart's rat face hovered into view,

pinched and white with fear. "Are you okay, Kobie?" He took my hand and patted it the way people in the movies did when somebody has fainted. "Say something! Are you hurt?"

I could not speak or move. I still sat in the chair, my legs hooked over the edge of the seat, the skirt of my dress hiked up my thighs. When I realized that, I tried to tug it into place. The other kids around us were snickering. Stuart got behind me and hefted the chair, with me in it, upright again. The numbness gradually left my arms and legs and, even though I had a roaring headache, I mustered the strength to swat at him.

"You're okay then." He went back to his seat and calmly began eating the cherry cobbler he'd turned down moments before, as if nothing had happened.

I trudged home that Friday afternoon with a lump on my head, a deep mistrust of anyone Stuart's size, an armload of homework, and a carton containing fifty Heath bars. The candy bars represented the measure of my despair; I had let myself be talked into taking a full box to sell over the weekend, as part of a drive to raise money for band uniforms.

In my room I tossed my books and the

candy bars on my unmade bed. Half the stuff bounced off to the floor. My room had not been cleaned since the day of Gretchen's accident. I didn't mind the mess, preferring to kick a path from the door to my bed. My mother harped day and night about the state of my filthy room, but considering the state of my mind, a dirty room seemed minor by comparison.

I didn't feel like doing homework right away and I certainly didn't feel like slogging through the snow to sell those stupid candy bars, so I went into my parents' room and called Gretchen.

Gretchen took forever coming to the phone and when she spoke, her voice was listless and unresponsive.

"What're you doing?" I asked, trying to bridge the enormous gap of silence that yawned between us.

"Nothing."

"How can you be doing nothing?" I insisted. "You must be doing *something*."

"I'm watching tv, Miss District Attorney. Is that all right with you?"

"You sure are touchy these days, Gretchen. I can't talk to you anymore."

"Maybe that's because we haven't much to say to each other. You go to Frost and I stay home. . . . You see all the kids at school and I don't see anybody but my tutor three days a week. We haven't got much in common, Kobie."

I felt a pluck of guilt. If it wasn't for me, Gretchen would be in school where she belonged. If only I had answered the chain letter, none of this would have happened. But I didn't tell her that.

"But, Gretchen, you're my best *friend*," I said, as if that solved everything.

Gretchen didn't rush right in and say "And you're *my* best friend" like she usually did. Instead she said she thought she heard her mother calling her and she'd have to hang up.

The evening loomed before me. I still didn't feel like tackling dreary old algebra, so I got out my drawing things. After clearing a space, I lay down on the floor with my inks and paper and the old *Life* magazine article and began copying a new scene from *Cinderella*. I discovered my sketching went faster than it used to, my fingers seemed more confident. Maybe all that notetaking and shorthand in history was paying off.

The carton of Heath bars sat directly in my line of vision. I stared at the orange and blue box as I cleaned the nib of my pen. I had never had a Heath bar before. I wondered what they looked like. I opened the carton and saw dozens of orange and blue wrapped candy bars stacked neatly inside. The delicious smell of chocolate nearly overwhelmed me.

It wouldn't hurt to eat *one*, I thought, just to see what it tasted like. I was supposed to sell the candy bars for fifty cents a piece. So I'd pay for the first one myself. No big deal. It was for a good cause. I unwrapped a candy bar and bit into it. Underneath the chocolate coating was a layer of crunchy butter toffee. I had never tasted anything so good in my whole life. Then I decided to sample another, just to see if it would be as good as the first. It was, maybe even a little better.

When my mother rapped on my door to call me to supper, I realized with alarm that I had eaten *ten* Heath bars. Quickly I swept the torn wrappers under my bed. At supper, I picked at the chicken and mashed potatoes on my plate, told my parents I wasn't very hungry (which was the truth), then went back to my room to work on my drawing. I ate three more Heath bars before I went to sleep.

Saturday morning I woke with a sense of dread. It was snowing outside, which made my room seem gloomier than ever. The pile of homework had managed to grow bigger overnight, too, like bread dough left in a pan to rise. I ate a Heath bar to give me energy to get out of bed, then another while I got dressed. I skipped brushing my teeth — I was just going to eat another Heath bar, so why bother?

And so it went the entire weekend. Shut in my messy room, I worked on my drawing, ignored my homework, ate Heath bars and very little else, and hated the world.

By Sunday night I had reached rock-bottom. Also the bottom of the Heath bar carton, where I found the card I was supposed to fill out totaling my candy bar sales. With my sugar-fogged brain, I slowly worked out how much I owed the school. Twenty-five dollars! I had eaten twenty-five dollars worth of candy in one weekend and all I had to show for it was a pile of orange and blue wrappers and a pale green face.

Yes, I was sick. Not the swift, hit-with-a-ton-of-bricks kind of sickness I got that time on the boardwalk with Gretchen, but a gradual, insidious, I'm-going-to-*die* kind of sickness brought on by fifty Heath bars consumed in less than three days and the knowledge I was in debt twenty-five dollars.

I staggered into the bathroom and hung over the toilet. I couldn't throw up. It was as if I was being punished for my greediness. I would probably be sick like this, but unable to declare it, for the rest of my life. Why couldn't I suddenly be struck with a serious illness so I would have to stay home from school a month or two? Why couldn't I have caught Stuart Buckley's rotten cold? I doubted I'd receive much sympathy for a Heath-bar binge.

Taking a wash cloth from the towel rack, I rinsed it in cold water and rubbed my clammy cheeks. My face in the mirror looked terrible.

"You've got to get hold of yourself," I ordered my pale green reflection. "You can't go on this way."

Tomorrow, I vowed, I would join the living. I would take Gretchen's long-ago advice and get into the swing of things. I would stop moping and feeling sorry for myself. And I would never, *ever*, eat another Heath bar even if tortured by the enemy.

One good thing about hitting rock-bottom: I had no place to go but up.

Chapter 11

"Kobie Roberts," Mr. Otte called from his seat in front of the stage. He leaned over to make a remark to Mr. Fernandez, the drama teacher, then checked my name off the list on his clipboard.

As I stumbled up the short flight of steps to the stage, I wondered whatever possessed me to sign the tryout sheet for *Oliver!* I couldn't sing or dance or act or even read cue cards without panicking at the thought of being in front of a real audience. Yet here I was, up on stage while the head music teacher and the drama teacher waited for me to announce my number. I blinked stupidly in the bright stage lights.

"What song are you doing, uh — Kobie, is it?" Mr. Otte asked, consulting his clipboard again.

"'I'd Do Anything For You,'" I whispered.

"What? We can't hear you," Mr. Fernandez said.

I cleared my throat, which had suddenly gotten a lump in it about the size and shape of a groundhog, a groundhog that refused to be dislodged from his hole no matter how many times I "a-hemmed." After two minutes of listening to me choke and gasp, like an old drain being unclogged, Miss Moncrief, the accompanist, brought me a paper cup of water.

"Drink this," she said. "And take a deep breath before you begin. Now, what are you singing?"

"'I'd Do Anything,'" I replied, after gulping the water.

"Good choice. Just get up there and belt it out," she encouraged. In a louder voice, so the two men in the front row could hear, she said, "Kobie is singing 'I'd Do Anything.'" Then she sat down at the piano and turned the pages of her music book to that selection. With her hands poised over the keyboard, she said to me, "Let me know when you're ready, Kobie."

I wouldn't be ready, I realized with a stab of icy fear, until 1999, but I didn't think the teachers would care to sit there that long. I still couldn't believe I was actually on stage, with the mimeographed sheet of the songs from *Oliver!* clasped in my sweaty hands. Acting upon my resolve to get into the swing of things at school, I had thought that trying out for *Oliver!* would be a nice, ambitious start. I'd decided to go for the female lead, Nancy, the waitress with a heart of gold. Gretchen had planned to try out for that part. I'd promised to help her with her lines back in November, but then she had had the accident.

Today was the last day for tryouts. I'd called my mother earlier and told her I was taking the late bus home. I thought all I'd have to do was read a few lines and Mr. Fernandez would give me the part on the spot. I found out too late that Nancy's role required a lot of singing and that in order to get the part, the drama and music teachers would not take my word for it that I could sing just fine — I had to perform in front of them and the other tryoutees.

I didn't have a bad voice — a sort of flat alto that sounded best when backed up with a forty-piece orchestra and a professional choir. Today, apparently, I didn't have any voice at all. I couldn't get anything to come out of my throat except croaks and coughs.

In the front row, Mr. Otte twiddled his

pencil impatiently, and behind him, a few kids giggled.

"Kobie," Miss Moncrief prodded gently. "Do you want to come back in a few minutes? Maybe someone else ought to go next —"

"No. I'm ready," I lied.

Miss Moncrief played the introductory bars, but when she got to the part where I was supposed to come in, I discovered my teeth were clamped together and I missed my cue. Miss Moncrief stopped and looked at me. The men in the front row gave a sigh that nearly ruffled the heavy velvet stage curtains.

"Sorry," I told Miss Moncrief. "My vocal cords are a little tight. I'll get it right this time."

She nodded and played the introduction again. I got the cue right this time, but the first note to leave my mouth came out as a high-pitched shriek. The teachers in the front row looked up at the ceiling, as if they expected to see the note flying around up there like a bird let out of its cage.

I couldn't seem to bring my voice back down to a normal level. I sang the entire song, plus choruses, in that awful fingernail-down-the-blackboard, eardrum-splitting screech. When I finished, I saw

Mr. Fernandez reach for his handkerchief and mop his forehead, as if he'd endured a terrible ordeal and was grateful it was finally over.

"Well!" Mr. Otte said. "I don't believe I've ever heard 'I'd Do Anything' sung in that particular key before. Interesting."

"I don't suppose you want me to read lines," I said dolefully.

"No," he replied, "I don't think that's necessary." He spoke briefly to Mr. Fernandez, who still hadn't recovered from my performance. "We've decided we could better use your — uh, talents elsewhere, Kobie. How would you like to work on costumes?"

"No! I mean, I wouldn't mind, except I'm a lousy sewer." To drive my point home, I added, "I sew even worse than I sing."

"I see." Mr. Fernandez thought a few seconds. "Well, we do need people to paint scenery. How are you with a paintbrush?"

"Okay, I guess." Painting scenery was a far cry from playing Nancy, but it was better than nothing.

"Good. I'll put you down for scenery, then. The scenery people meet Friday after school." Mr. Otte checked his list, obviously eager to get me off the stage.

I was only too happy to comply. Thanking Miss Moncrief for her help, I hurried down the steps, gathered my books and coat from my chair, and was about to leave the cafeteria when I heard Mr. Otte call out, "Stuart Buckley."

Stuart had been sitting on the other side of the cafeteria. He stumped up on the stage and told Miss Moncrief the number he had chosen to sing.

"Is your cold better, Stuart?" Mr. Otte asked him. "I'd hate to hear you at less than your best." After my stage debut, he was probably a little leery of singers who weren't prepared.

"I'm fine," Stuart said. "I'm going to do 'Where Is Love?'"

"When you're ready."

I sat down again, not wanting to miss this for the world. Stuart had listened to my dreadful performance and I was sure he'd razz me plenty over it. I wanted to catch his act so I'd have ammunition to fire back.

I was stunned when Stuart began singing. He sang Oliver's ballad so plaintively, so wistfully, I could almost see him wearing the orphan's rags, trying to find love in harsh Victorian London. When the last sad notes died away, I felt tears gathering in my eyes. Stuart — locker-slamming, chair-kicking, beastly little Stuart — was simply wonderful.

If Mr. Otte thought so, too, he never let on. "Sing something else, Stuart. How about 'Consider Yourself'?"

Stuart launched into the Artful Dodger's song with zest and gusto, using the Dodger's boastful gestures as he strutted back and forth. When he finished, he exited stage right and came over to where I was sitting.

"You were terrific," I told him honestly. "I'm sure you'll get the part of Oliver Twist."

He shrugged, typically. "Oh, I don't know. I'll probably get to be one of the workhouse orphans. Thanks, anyway. You weren't half-bad yourself."

"Oh, come on, Stuart. I was terrible. I'm surprised they didn't throw rotten eggs and yank me off with a hook." I picked up my books, a little uncomfortable to find us having an ordinary conversation. "I'm painting scenery, as you heard, so I'll get to watch you rehearse."

"Yeah, sure." He looked uneasily toward the stage, and I wondered if he was remembering the day of the dance when he'd made a play for me on that very same stage. "Well, see you around."

I left the cafeteria and walked down the

hall. As I passed the art room, I heard Mrs. Ryerson call out, "Kobie! Kobie, dear, I'm so glad to see you!"

"You are?" I couldn't believe anybody was glad to see me after my tryout, except maybe an ear-plug salesman who could have cleaned up while I was on stage singing.

"Come in, dear." Mrs. Ryerson fluttered over to the doorway and ushered me inside. "It's just wonderful, Kobie. I can't tell you how thrilled I am to see such beautiful work. I always said you had great promise."

Surely she wasn't talking about my audition. But then I knew she wasn't, because she guided me over to a work table, where, spread out from end to end, were my Disney drawings.

"How did — ?" And then it came to me. Only one person besides me had the combination to my locker. Only one person knew of the existence of the plastic insurance envelope on the top shelf and what it contained. And only one person had the nerve to break into my locker and steal the drawings, even if he was only going to show them to my art teacher.

"A boy in one of my other classes brought this envelope up to my desk today. He said he found it on the floor and that

I ought to take a look at what was inside, that somebody was letting a lot of talent go to waste," Mrs. Ryerson explained. "I didn't get a chance to look until after my last class."

"This boy, does he come up to about here —" I indicated a point several inches below my chin "— and wear glasses?"

"Why, yes. That's Stuart all right. Do you know him?"

"Sort of."

"Well, he certainly did me a favor. Why didn't you show me these before, Kobie?"

"Really, Mrs. Ryerson, I didn't want to bother you with my pictures. They aren't very good —"

"What are you saying, Kobie? Of course, they're very good. They're magnificent. I want to see more."

"Well, I haven't drawn for quite a while. I only have one other picture I did over the weekend." Just the mention of the infamous Heath-bar weekend was enough to make my stomach pitch and roll.

"Bring it in, bring it in," Mrs. Ryerson said. "Now, the important thing is to give you time to develop your drawing skills, since your true gift clearly lies in that area. I'm going to excuse you from all other art projects until the end of the year, to let you concentrate on your drawing."

I couldn't believe what I was hearing. "I get to draw the rest of the year? My own stuff, like these?"

"Whatever you want. You're interested in animation, aren't you?" She went over to her bookcase and rummaged through a pile of magazines. "Ah, here it is. You might want to take a look at this."

The art magazine she gave me was turned to an article on animation, with loads of pictures from Disney movies. There was a whole section on *Cinderella* alone.

"This is great, Mrs. Ryerson. Can I take this home?"

"Certainly. Tomorrow, Kobie, I'm going to set up a drawing table in that corner for you. That's where you'll keep your things. And of course you can use any supplies you need." She indicated my heavily-crayoned mouse from *Cinderella*, the one that bore a remarkable resemblance to Stuart. "We don't have the special paints animators use, because they work on celluloid, but we do have watercolors and acrylics, which are better than crayons. And I want you to take this home and get used to using it."

She unlocked a drawer in her desk and took out a pen and a bottle of ink. "This is a Rapidograph pen. You'll find it has a finer, smoother line than those laundry markers you've been using. It's a very expensive instrument, Kobie, so be very careful."

I took the pen as if it were the Hope diamond and put it in my purse. "I won't let it out of my sight, Mrs. Ryerson," I promised. "Thanks a lot."

"I hope you realize I'm giving you this time because I think you show promise."

"I know. I'm really — I don't know what to say."

"Don't say anything. Just make me proud. You will do one finished drawing for your final grade." She smiled. "See you tomorrow, Kobie. Be ready to work."

I sailed out of the art room on winged feet, with the Rapidograph pen in my purse and a bright, silvery hope in my heart that, starting tomorrow, my great talent would finally be unleashed upon an unsuspecting world.

Chapter 12

The Rapidograph pen was the dickens to fill with ink and very tricky to use, but once I got the hang of it, drawings and sketches fairly flew off my private table in the art room. Sixth period became a shining oasis in the dull landscape of my day. I was blissfully happy, in art class at least, for the first time all year.

After Mrs. Ryerson had encouraged me to do what I wanted, I regretted my rash decision to paint scenery for the spring play and dreaded the first Friday meeting. I hated organized activities — clubs, groups, committees, even meeting two other people on a street corner — because rules and regulations and bylaws always made me feel locked in, trapped. I envisioned scenery painters slavishly toiling over the backdrops, with only a one-minute break in which to straighten up.

I was wrong. The sweat shop I had pictured turned out to be more like a free-for-all. We were rather loosely organized by Mr. Fernandez, the drama teacher, who didn't care if we slapped paint on each other or swung from the rafters, just as long as the backdrops were done right. We horsed around as much as we worked, which was fun, plus we got to watch rehearsals.

Stuart Buckley did not win the part of Oliver. Gretchen's ex-boyfriend Jake got it. Stuart was the Artful Dodger, a role that suited his fiendish instincts more than goody-goody Oliver Twist. Midge of the perfect hair and quavering soprano won the role of Nancy, naturally. And Julia Neal played Bet. Since her part was not very big or demanding, Julia also asked to be on the backdrop committee. This surprised me because I thought Julia was too finicky to lower herself to a task as menial as painting scenery.

But Julia herself was a surprise. She *wanted* to work with me, because she thought I was such a great artist, so we often painted side by side, talking and joking, with none of the animosity that had marked our previous dealings. I found that Julia and a lot of the other people were actually very nice, and I looked forward to Fridays after school as much as I did sixth periods.

The only tarnished spot in my bright new life was Gretchen. When I called her to tell her about my disastrous tryout and to let her know I had taken her advice and gotten into the swing of things at last, she didn't act at all pleased.

"Painting scenery isn't so great," she said petulantly. "Who's going to know what you painted? It isn't like getting up on stage and acting."

"*I'll* know what I've painted and, anyway, there were only so many parts to go around. We couldn't all be actors," I said. "Jake is Oliver Twist, probably because he's so cute."

"Good for him," she sniffed. "Who's Nancy?" I knew that was the part she'd wanted before the accident.

"Midge Murphy, who else? You would have been much better in the role, Gretch. She sings almost as badly as I do and she can't remember her lines from one second to the next. Everybody from the stage hands to the director has to feed her lines to her." I rattled on, thinking she wanted to hear all about the play. "Stuart is the Artful Dodger, which is just perfect for him. Nobody likes him and they give him a tough time, but he doesn't seem to let it get in the way of his acting. Mr. Fernandez says he's a real professional. Oh, and Julia works with me on scenery."

"Julia? I thought you didn't like Julia," Gretchen said, almost accusingly.

"I don't like Julia with Midge but Julia without Midge is just fine. I think Midge is a bad influence on her. Before I forget, I wanted to tell you about the assembly we had the other day. You missed the funniest — "

"I don't want to hear about school stuff anymore," Gretchen broke in. "It's boring. School, school, school. I mean, who cares?"

I guess to her it sounded like I was bragging about all the things I was doing at Frost. I thought she would have been thrilled I was part of the in-crowd — well, at least part of the *fringes* of the in-crowd. Gretchen was so unpredictable these days.

"You're right," I said, changing the subject. "School is a terrible bore. I would have quit long ago, except my mother makes me go. I can't wait till summer, can you?"

"Yes, I can. I have another surgery, remember?"

"Oh, yeah. I forgot." It seemed I couldn't say anything that didn't aggravate Gretchen one way or another. "Well, enough about me. What's new with you?"

"Nothing. Absolutely nothing. The tutor

comes three days a week. And I go to the doctor every other week. Very exciting."

I tried to make light conversation but it was like rolling a boulder uphill. Gretchen was so down I hung up without telling her my best news of all, the fact that Mrs. Ryerson was letting me do my own project in art class.

As February trickled into March, our phone conversations dwindled more and more. Sometimes a whole week would go by and I'd realize with a twinge of guilt that I hadn't called Gretchen. She almost never called me. If I hadn't been so busy at school, I would have felt hurt. But I had Stuart and Julia and the other kids working on the play to talk to, so the full effect of Gretchen's snub was blunted somewhat.

I was still stuck with Stuart during lunch. The new friendliness between Julia and me did not extend to a seat at Midge's table, but even that was okay. Stuart and I talked about the play, instead of bickering constantly, and I only had to yell at him a few times for getting out of line. He never mentioned that time backstage at the dance and I never brought up the subject of his new stepmother.

At home, I spent a lot of time in my

157

room, copying movie scenes from the article Mrs. Ryerson had lent me and working on preliminary sketches for my end-of-the-year project. I didn't clean my room but I didn't fight with my mother much, either. In fact, I didn't talk much to either of my parents. I began to feel like a boarder in my own house, but it wasn't such a bad feeling, this being independent.

So I was shocked when I came home from school one rainy day in April to have my mother meet me at the door with hot chocolate and a big grin.

"What's up?" I asked, immediately suspicious. "Did you win the lottery or something?"

"Why don't you go in your room and find out?" she replied cryptically.

I opened the door of my bedroom, expecting to see a wrecking crew demolishing the place or authorities from reform school packing my clothes. I did *not* expect to see a brand-new record player sitting on the floor.

My mother was right behind me. I whirled around. "Is this mine? Is it really, really mine?"

"Of course, it's yours. Would I put something I bought for myself in your room? I might never see it again." But there was no sting in her words. She laughed at my confusion. "Go on, Kobie. Plug it in. Let's hear how it sounds."

I was too flabbergasted to move. "But why? I mean, it's not my birthday. Not for months yet."

"Well, it *is* your birthday present. Early. I'm sure you don't mind getting it ahead of time. I know you were hoping to get a record player for Christmas, since you bought that record, but I had already bought you the coat. I found this on sale at Robinson's and put it on layaway last month."

"Why are you giving it to me now?"

She came over to ruffle my hair. "Well, you've been down in the dumps lately. What with Gretchen's accident and her not coming back to school. You've been so quiet, spending so much time in your room, I thought you needed something to cheer you up. So I told your father this morning I was getting the record player out of layaway early and he said it was a good idea. And here it is. Do you like it?"

Why was it when somebody did something nice for me I always felt rotten to the core with guilt? I didn't deserve to get this wonderful present. Not after the way I'd argued with my mother about my clothes and my room and a million other things. How many times had I complained that I wished we were rich, whenever I wanted something and my mother had said we couldn't afford it? I thought of the time I'd carried on at the shopping center and had made my mother buy me that outfit and the time she'd made my miniskirt so I could wear it to the dance and the time she'd worked an entire weekend fixing my home ec project so I'd at least get a passing grade. I remembered she had advanced my allowance so I could pay for those stupid candy bars. I felt sniveling and wretched and undeserving of anything beyond an iron cot without sheets and a diet of stale bread and water.

"Don't you like it?" my mother asked, a little put out by my lack of reaction. "I don't know much about record players, but the man at the store said this was a good buy. It has a good sound and an automatic something-or-other that changes the records. He said it was perfect for a girl your age."

"It is! Oh, Mom, I love it! Thanks a lot!" I gave her a hug, which she tentatively returned. We both felt a little strange, I think. We hadn't hugged in ages.

She handed me a bag that contained the instruction booklet and an album that came free with the record player — a selection of Christmas songs sung by people no one had ever heard of. I plugged it in, set the automatic changer, and we both watched as the Christmas record dropped down and the tone arm automatically went over and sat gently down on the revolving record. It was like magic. When "Joy to the World" came blasting out of the speakers, we both jumped, then laughed. I turned down the volume.

My mother listened a few minutes. "So you like it then?"

"It's great, Mom. Absolutely perfect. I couldn't have picked out a better one myself." I jumped up from the floor where I had been watching the record go around and around. "I can't wait to tell Gretchen. I'm going to call her right now."

"Maybe you'd better wait a while, Kobie."

"Why? Why should I wait?"

"Well, Gretchen might not want to hear about your getting your birthday present early," she said.

"I don't see why not. She already has a record player. Now we both have one."

"I know and ordinarily she'd be thrilled, but — well, her mother told me she's having such a terrible time adjusting to her injuries. I just think you ought to wait a bit."

I took into consideration the way

Gretchen had been acting lately. "Okay. I'll wait until she calls me and then maybe I'll slip it in the conversation."

When my mother left to start supper, I reached under the dresser and pulled out my Byrds album. At long, long last, I could play my record. I tore off the shrink-wrap and set the automatic changer so the Christmas album would stop playing and the Byrds album would drop down on top of it. I held my breath as the tone arm glided over and set down feather-light on the record.

The first jangly notes of "Mr. Tambourine Man" vibrated from the speakers, the twelve-string guitar followed by the deep throbbing bass and the rhythmic tambourine. I closed my eyes and sang along with the lead singer.

"He-ey, Mr. Tambourine Man, play
    a song for me.
I'm not sleepy and there ain't no place
    I'm going to.
Hey-ey, Mr. Tambourine Man, play a
    song for me.
In the jingle-jangle mornin', I'll come
    followin' you."

Instantly, I was back at the beach house at Ocean City with Gretchen. I could smell her nail polish and feel the sand under my feet. I could feel the sun-dried starchiness of my cut-offs and hear the surf *shu-shushing*. Something in my chest squeezed tight the way it had when I'd first heard the song over Gretchen's transistor radio.

I remembered us racing up the board-walk, dodging people as we crammed down french fries. I remembered the dusty semidarkness of the penny arcade and could hear the mechanical wheezes and groans of Madame Zaza as she issued each of us a little white card, sealing our fates for the year. I remembered the other-world strangeness under the boardwalk as Gretchen had snuggled up to Dwayne, and the faint strains of my song coming from yet another radio.

Until now, last summer had seemed as if it were a hundred years ago. "Mr. Tam-bourine Man" brought it all spinning back.

I lay down on the floor and put my head in my arms, letting the music wash over me. And then I remembered something else. The first time I rode up an escalator without my mother. We had gotten sepa-rated and she was waiting impatiently for me at the top. I had clung to the rail for dear life, watching the steps flatten and become silvery grids that disappeared into a crack as I neared the top.

"Get ready to step off," my mother had instructed from above. "Pay attention, Kobie."

I *had been* paying attention. In fact, I had been terrified that I would flatten like one of the steps and slip through the crack, quick as an envelope through a letter slot. As I had approached the top, my feet had seemed glued to the step and I hadn't wanted to get off, but I knew I had no choice. When my turn came, I would have to pick up my feet and get off.

That was the feeling I'd experienced when I'd first heard "Mr. Tambourine Man" at the beach house last summer. I had the same feeling now. Turning thirteen, I realized, was like riding the escalator to a new floor. In a way I'd been in a hurry to get there. Yet as I had gotten closer, I hadn't been so anxious to get off. But now I had to.

I played my record over and over, not even getting up to switch on the lights, until my mother called me to supper.

Chapter 13

When Mrs. Shufflebarger handed out copies of the yearbook in homeroom, I knew the school year was over, never mind that we still had a week and a half to go. I stared at the cover of "A Passing Glimpse." The other kids in class were already noisily signing each others' yearbooks. I knew nobody would ask to sign mine, so I took my time leafing through it.

The front page photograph of Dr. Smyth, the principal, confirmed the man really did exist. The principal was seen so seldom, I often speculated he was a fictitious character the administration made up just to keep us in line. I located my teachers' pictures: Mrs. Vandenheuvel at the lectern; my math teacher, Mr. Blister, looking long-suffering, as usual; Mrs. Ryerson working on a painting; Mrs. Humphrey with her arm buried in the sleeve of somebody's dress (probably mine) and looking as if she'd been stuck by pins.

After the teachers came the class pictures. Stuart Buckley wore the faintest smile, as if he'd just given the photographer a hot foot. Midge Murphy's hair was absolutely perfect; in the row below her, Julia Neal grinned at the camera. In my own picture, I looked only slightly less stupid than Jo Ann Holford, who was without question the geekiest girl in school. Then I remembered to look up Gretchen. As I turned the pages, I wondered if we'd had our class pictures taken before or after her accident. And there she was, wearing her madras jumper and her familiar smile, the smile I had not seen in a long time.

"Kobie." Julia nudged my arm. She held out her yearbook, opened to a page already crammed with names. "Sign my yearbook?"

"Sure," I said, managing to hide my surprise. "If you'll do mine." We swapped yearbooks and I chewed on my pen thoughtfully as if I was trying to think of something meaningful to say. Actually, I was reading all the other comments in Julia's yearbook. "With love from me to you, Guess who?", Remember the football game at Lanier!!!"

Julia signed mine swiftly and was ready

to hand it back while I was still hunting for a place to write. I found a spot on the inside back cover and scribbled, after weighty deliberation, "To a great scenery-painter, don't ever forget the spring play, Kobie." It wasn't exactly a quote that would ever be immortalized on a monument, but I hoped it would remind Julia that we were friends, sort of.

She took her yearbook without looking at what I had written. "Thanks," she said and was off to nab a few more signatures before the bell.

I peeked at what she had scrawled on the pristine whiteness of the inside cover of my yearbook. Julia had opted for the safe, generic, "To a real sweet kid, good luck at Woodson."

Stuart hadn't ordered a yearbook but he was quite eager to deface mine. "Let me sign it," he said at lunch and I handed my yearbook over to him, my heart sinking.

Stuart hid whatever he was doing behind his math book and it wasn't until fourth period that I had a chance to look at the mess he had made of my yearbook.

He had drawn devil's horns and a beard over his own picture, which was certainly apt, and sketched a balloon over the picture of the dumbest boy in school, Arthur Pearsall, saying I was his dream girl. Stuart had also inscribed, in different handwritings, the inside covers with such gems as "Don't ever kiss by the garden gate, love is blind but the neighbors ain't."

I sighed. Some things never change.

"Finished your project?" Mrs. Ryerson asked, stopping by my drawing table. "I'm dying to see what you've done."

I untied the tapes of the cardboard portfolio Mrs. Ryerson had lent me so I could take my drawings home without getting them dirty. "I hope you like them," I said nervously. "I've been working on them for days."

"Yes, you've been working hard and it shows," Mrs. Ryerson said. "Did you do a scene from *Cinderella*?"

"Two scenes actually," I told her. "I couldn't choose between two so I did them both."

I lifted the cover of the portfolio, holding my breath expectantly as the first drawing came into view.

Mrs. Ryerson's face broke into a delighted grin. "Oh, Kobie — !"

"I did this one because I liked the composition, but it was harder to do than it looks," I explained. I had drawn my Stuart-mouse trapped in a rain pipe. The ever-narrowing concentric circles of the rain pipe filled the entire picture, with the Stuart-mouse at the bottom, crying to get out. The thought of stuffing Stuart in a rain pipe had given me hours of pleasure.

"It's wonderful," Mrs. Ryerson acknowledged. "The light and shading are just right. I know how difficult that was to do."

"And then I did this one." I flipped to the next drawing, a scene where Cinderella's fairy godmother is turning the pumpkin into the golden coach. Cinderella and her mouse friends are watching as the tendrils of pumpkin vines are about to become the wheels of the coach. I was especially proud of my fairy dust effect, hundreds of tiny white stars painstakingly etched over the midnight-blue background.

"This is very good, too," my teacher said. "But I thought you'd do the scene of Cinderella at the ball."

She referred to the art magazine picture of Cinderella at the ball with her prince, holding hands by a fountain. You could almost hear the gurgle of the aqua water splashing into the star-spangled pool.

"I know," I said. "I fooled around with a few sketches, but I couldn't get the water right." That wasn't entirely true. I had purposely chosen to draw the pumpkin-into-coach scene because I liked the idea of capturing that split-second instant of magic when anything could happen.

Mrs. Ryerson took my drawings over to the window to study them in better light. "I always believed you had talent. One of these days, I'm going to see your name listed among the animators of a Walt Disney movie."

"I hope so. Oh, I almost forgot. Here's your pen back. I took good care of it." I dug the Rapidograph pen out of my purse.

"What pen?" she said, giving me a big wink, and I knew she meant for me to keep it. I was going to miss Mrs. Ryerson when I went to Woodson High next year and I told her so.

I went home that afternoon with Mrs. Ryerson's praises ringing in my ears.

"Don't faint," I warned my mother. "I'm going to clean my room."

"And without my nagging you. Too bad, I was looking forward to it." Since seeing the play *Oliver!* my mother thought workhouses for children were a fine idea.

I laughed. I was beginning to see that my mother was a real person, with a sense of humor, just like me. She wasn't so bad, even when she *was* nagging me.

I had taken both my parents to the opening night of *Oliver!* My father had been so proud to see my name in the program, lumped with all the other scenery-painters, he had pointed it out to everyone sitting around us. And whenever the backdrop had changed, my mother had asked loudly what part I had worked on. The show was a great success, mostly due to Stuart as the Artful Dodger. It was a nice feeling to know I had contributed to the production, even if I had only painted the staircase in the workhouse scene or the five row houses in the street scene.

My mother followed me to my room. "Why the sudden change of heart? Can't find your bed anymore?" she teased, and I didn't mind.

"I need to find space for my record player, get it off the floor. And I want to fix a place for my drawing stuff. I'm going to draw all summer. Mrs. Ryerson says I have great talent."

She didn't comment on this. "Gretchen's mother called me today," she said instead.

I hadn't talked to Gretchen in ages. "Nothing's wrong, is it?" I asked, bending to pick up shoes and books.

"No, not exactly. She wanted to know if it would be all right to go to the beach early this year."

The beach. I had totally forgotten about our annual week at Ocean City. "We're going *early*?"

She nodded. "The last of the month, before Gretchen's surgery in August. At first they weren't going at all, but Clare told me she thought Gretchen really needs a little vacation."

"I don't know why," I said with sudden bitterness. "This whole year's been a vacation for her. She's gotten out of everything."

"Kobie Roberts, what on earth is the matter with you? Gretchen has had a terrible time. There's no call for such talk. And for your information, Gretchen hasn't gotten out of anything. She has to repeat the eighth grade next year."

I looked up, stunned. "She does? Why? I thought she was being tutored."

"Her tutor couldn't take Gretchen's tests for her. Gretchen didn't do well in about half her subjects. That's why she's being left back. Clare says she's terribly upset — now she won't start high school with her friends."

Her friends . . . and me, her *best* friend. I would have to face high school next year without Gretchen. I dropped a handful of papers into the trash can, depressed at the prospect. Gretchen repeating eighth grade, staying behind at Frost while I went on to Woodson — and it was all my fault.

My mother stared at me. "Don't take it so hard, Kobie. I know it's a blow, but

Gretchen's the one being held back, not you."

"You don't understand," I said miserably. "She flunked because of me."

"What are you talking about?"

I told her about the chain letter I decided not to answer the day of Gretchen's accident. "The letter said something awful would happen if I broke the chain and it did!"

My mother cleared a chair and made me sit down. "In the first place," she said carefully, "chain letters are superstitious nonsense. Gretchen's accident did *not* happen because of something you did."

"Then why *did* it happen? Suppose I had answered the stupid letter like I was supposed to and she didn't have the accident — "

"And suppose she did?" my mother threw back. "You can't foretell the future, Kobie. Nobody can. I'm not sure I'd even want to. Why Gretchen had that accident is something I can't answer, but I do know you had nothing whatsoever to do with it."

I slumped in the chair. "I bet Gretchen really hates me now. I'm going on to high school and she'll be stuck at Frost another year."

"I know it'll be hard on your friendship," my mother said, surprising me. I never thought she paid attention to anything going on. "I'm not sure I would have handled this the way Clare has."

"You mean if I had been hurt instead of Gretchen?"

"I would have made you go back to school, instead of staying home."

"Even if I didn't want to go?"

"We don't always get what we want in this world and that's part of Gretchen's problem. Her mother is too soft." She pursed her lips, as if realizing she'd said too much. "Forget about that business with the chain letter, Kobie."

I was certainly willing to forget about it, but Madame Zaza's predictions at Ocean City last summer weren't so easily dismissed. Gretchen's card had actually *said* dark days were ahead for her. Even if I wasn't responsible for Gretchen's accident by ignoring the chain letter, there was still the matter of my card and the room without mirrors business.

Gretchen and I were tied together. Whatever happened to her affected me.

The last day of school arrived. I received the brown envelope containing my report cards, one from each teacher, in homeroom. By some miracle, every one of my teachers promoted me to the ninth grade.

"See you this fall," Julia said as we left to go to an abbreviated first period. The last day of school was only a half-day, without lunch served. "I'll be looking for you at Woodson. Have a nice summer!"

"I will," I said, pleased that Julia had promised to look me up next year. "You, too."

The morning flew by and then the final bell rang. The bell was drowned out by a roar like the Hoover Dam bursting. Kids raced down the hall like escaped convicts, waving their report cards.

Stuart lounged in front of locker 1473, which he had already opened. I didn't have much in there, since we had turned in our books earlier in the week.

"You still here?" I asked him. "I thought you'd be the first one on the bus."

"I'll be glad to get out of this dump, you got that right."

"I take it you passed."

He grinned. "I don't think my teachers could survive another day with me in their classes. What about you?"

"I passed, no thanks to you. It's a good thing Woodson is a big school. Next year I probably won't even see you."

"I'll find you. Who else will show you the ropes?"

"And who else will drive me crazy?" In

a more civil tone I said, "Well, it's been interesting, Stuart, I'll have to say that. Working on the play was fun."

"And sharing lunches, don't forget that."

"You never said, but I'm going to ask anyhow — whatever happened between you and your parents? Did your grandmother get custody of you?"

"Not yet. It takes a while. But I'm sure she will because my father said *he* doesn't want me and I know his wife doesn't. Don't worry, Kobie, my grandmother lives close by. I'll be going to Woodson." He paused. "You never said, but I'm going to ask about your friend. The one who was in the car wreck? You never talk about her."

"She's okay. Mostly. She has to come back here next year, though. She flunked."

"Tough."

"Yeah." I collected the few papers and stray pencils from the bottom of my locker. I nodded toward the door Stuart was swinging on. "Go ahead. For old time's sake."

"For old time's sake." He slammed the locker with a bang like a pistol shot.

I held out my hand. "Good luck at Woodson, Stuart."

"Same to you, Kobie." He shook my hand solemnly.

Eighth grade was over.

Chapter 14

Our beach house looked the same as ever. The cabbage rose linoleum in our second floor apartment was still gritty with sand. Through the glass-doored cupboards I could see the same green glass dishes we had used year after year.

The only thing different was that the third floor garret was empty. We had rented the house earlier this year, June instead of August, before the season really started. I was a little disappointed. Spying on the bachelor in the garret was a tradition that died hard. No matter how old I get, I suppose I'll always be curious.

In the past, Gretchen and I would throw our stuff down and run to the beach first thing, while our parents would putter around with agonizing slowness, unpacking the groceries and even scrubbing already-clean bathrooms and kitchenettes.

I didn't really know what to expect from Gretchen this year. We had come in separate cars — for the first time, Gretchen and I hadn't whined hysterically to ride in the same car. My folks arrived at the beach house first, though both families had left at the same time from my house. I changed into my bathing suit in the closet that served as my bedroom. While I was fastening the straps of my old yellow two-piece, I heard Gretchen and her parents banging into the apartment below. I sat on the bed and pulled tufts out of the old chenille spread, giving them time to get settled.

When I went downstairs, figuring Gretchen was not going to come up to get *me*, I saw her standing uncertainly by the sleeping porch, as if she'd been debating whether or not to come upstairs. She had on a new Hang Ten bikini that made the most of her curves.

"Hi, Gretch. I like your suit," I said. If I had outgrown mine, I would have gotten a new one, too, but the top piece *still* fit a little loose.

"Oh, hi, Kobie. I can't believe we're finally here. Daddy had to fix a flat on the way."

Gretchen's mother was in the kitchen, putting away groceries. She waved at me. "Why don't you girls go on down to the beach? We'll be down in a little while."

"You want to?" I asked Gretchen.

"I guess. Only I can't get my face in the sun. I have to wear this stuff." She threw a tube into her beach bag and picked up the straw hat lying next to it. "What time do you want us back?" she called to her mother. "One hour? Two?"

Mrs. Farris came out on the porch. "I think you girls are old enough to use your own judgment. Check in before dinnertime — we might go out tonight. Gretch, be sure to wear your hat. Remember what the doctor said."

"Gosh, we can stay out all day," I remarked as we walked the short block to the beach. In our new-found independence, we didn't have to pant and run around the way we used to, rushing to use our allotted free time. Now I knew why grown-ups never bothered to hurry; they had all the time in the world.

We spread our towels on the sand, angled to catch the sun and a good view of the lifeguard stand. Gretchen smeared white goo from the tube on her face, then clumped the straw hat on her head. "I hate this dumb hat," she said. "I look like I'm at least ninety."

With her figure? "Don't worry, Gretch. The last thing the boys will notice is your hat," I said truthfully. "Why can't you get your face tan?"

"It's bad for my skin. My doctor says I'll probably never be able to get my face sunburned after I have that skin graft."

We sat on our towels, watching people playing in the ocean and not saying much. Things were still strained between us. I wondered if we would ever be as close as we used to be.

Somewhere behind us a radio played the latest number one hit. I thought how "Mr. Tambourine Man" had jangled from everybody's radios last summer. Another year, another song. Suddenly the Froot Loop fad and miniskirts that had ruled the eighth grade seemed a long time ago.

I saw the boy first. He was walking along the surf line, creating a sensation, oblivious that females of all ages were swooning in his wake. He had long, sun-streaked hair and a tan that could have only been acquired by a winter in Tahiti. Nobody was that tan so early in the summer.

"Gretchen! Look at that! Did you ever see anything so gorgeous?"

She sat up and followed my gaze. "No, I haven't. I'm not sure he's real. How long have we been out in the sun?"

"If he's a mirage, then we've all seen

the same one," I said, indicating an entire beach of women and girls who were sitting up, shading their eyes to watch the progress of Golden Boy.

"He's going to pass us," she whispered, as if he could hear us. "And here I am with this ridiculous hat on! He won't look at me twice!"

She was worried about a hat? At least she wasn't wearing a bathing suit that only looked good on an eight-year-old. I realized then that Gretchen was letting the scar on her face rule her life. "Listen, Gretch, with your figure and that suit, the rest of us might as well go throw ourselves in the ocean. Besides, the hat makes you look mysterious."

"Really?" She thought this over. "I read somewhere that men like mysterious women."

"There you go," I said. "Maybe I'll get a hat, too, and a mustache and maybe a long gray beard down to my knees. Think that'll be mysterious enough?"

That cracked her up. We were both laughing when Golden Boy passed our towels. He didn't notice either one of us.

After lying in the sun an hour or so, we got restless.

"Want to go up on the boardwalk?" I suggested. "I need to buy a T-shirt."

"Okay." Gretchen got up and began shaking the sand from her towel. "I'm dying of thirst, too."

The boardwalk was fairly crowded with midafternoon shoppers like us, who were tired of the hot sun. In the Thunderbird Shop, we each bought oversized white T-shirts that we put on over our bathing suits. Gretchen bought a pair of aviator-style sunglasses.

"I'm supposed to keep the glare out of my eyes," she said. "I can't stand this clip-on thing the doctor gave me to stick on my regular glasses." She put her heavy, black-framed glasses and the clip-ons into her beach bag and tried on her new sunglasses. "I don't care if I can't see very well. At least I look better."

"You look just like a movie star," I said, because she did. I would have bought sunglasses, too, but in order for me to look like a movie star, the sunglasses would have had to cover me from head to toe, like a diving bell. But I did find a beautiful copper bracelet, the kind open in the middle so you could squeeze it on your wrist. The bracelet hung rather loosely around my birdbone wrist but I still loved it.

Sporting our new finery, we went to Snicks 'N Snacks and sat on the stools at the wooden counter while we split an order of french fries and drank Cokes. I reminded Gretchen of the time I got sick on the boardwalk.

"We were both so *juvenile* back then," she remarked, lapsing into last year's vocabulary.

"You'll be fourteen next week," I said. "And I'll be fourteen at the end of July. Thirteen was a long year for me."

"For you? What about me?" She drained her Coke in a noisy clatter of ice cubes.

"For both of us," I said firmly. I wanted to reestablish a feeling of equality between us, to acknowledge we'd *both* had a difficult year but we could start fourteen off on the right foot, if we worked at being best friends again. The thing was, I wasn't sure Gretchen even *wanted* to be best friends anymore.

We ambled up the boardwalk, toward the amusements. When we came to the penny arcade, we stopped and looked at each other, both remembering the fortune cards from Madame Zaza.

"Want to go in?" Gretchen asked.

"Why not? Play you a game of skeetball." I sounded nonchalant, but was in fact a little anxious. This was where our fates for the past year had been decided, and they were dillies.

The penny arcade was murky, lit only by

flashing pinball machines. There were a couple of younger kids fooling around, but otherwise the place was empty. Somehow we found ourselves in front of Madame Zaza's glass booth. The mechanical fortune-teller was silent, waiting for someone to drop a coin in the slot below her crystal ball. In the smoky, dim interior of the arcade, I felt the same shaky powerlessness I had experienced last summer, only without the nausea.

Gretchen put her hand on my arm. "It didn't have anything to do with what happened," she said.

"But the cards — "

"It was just coincidence. Charles hit a slick spot on the road and that's all. Those cards are like fortune cookies — they don't mean a thing."

I looked at her. She had taken off her sunglasses when we'd come in and didn't seem so cool and unreachable. "Gretch, I've been so miserable. All I could think was that somehow it was my fault — "

"I know. I thought that, too, for a while. Not that it was your fault, but that if we hadn't gotten our fortunes told — " She broke off, then said, "Let's get out of here, okay?"

On our way out of the arcade, we passed a bank of trick mirrors. Naturally we had to stop and giggle at our reflections.

"Hallelujah! I finally got a figure!" I exclaimed as I wiggled my nonexistent hips. The mirror made me look curvy. We laughed like hyenas as we saw ourselves short and fat, tall and skinny, pear-shaped, and just plain distorted.

The last mirror was regular but it had been tinted so dark that our reflections stared out at us like strangers from another planet where everything was identical, but shadowed. We stood there a moment, transfixed by our images.

"That's us, last year," Gretchen said quietly. The depth of her insight astonished me. She was right; we were looking at our former selves, two people who had spent their thirteenth year in rooms without mirrors, avoiding seeing ourselves as we really were. In a way, Madame Zaza's predictions had come true for us both.

I felt Gretchen's eyes in the shadow mirror and realized that she was more than just a friend — she was my other half. She must have realized it, too, because she said earnestly, "Kobie, I hope we never stop being friends. I was so miserable this past year."

"Me, too. Nothing was the same without you." I thought for a second we were going to cry, right there in public.

"It'll be even tougher next year. You'll be going on to Woodson and I'll be stuck at Frost."

"We'll still ride the same bus," I said. "And we'll see each other after school and talk on the phone just like always."

"I'll work extra hard to catch up," Gretchen promised rashly. "Maybe I can cram two semesters into one."

We walked out of the penny arcade. The sun was just starting to dip behind the beach houses. "I guess we'd better go back and see what our parents are up to," I said. "They've probably lost all track of the time. You know how it is when they get older."

"I know what you mean. My father took so long to change the flat on our way up here, it would have been faster to buy a new car."

We were heading down the boardwalk when Gretchen suddenly shrieked, "There he is!" I knew instantly who she meant — Gretchen's cute-boy radar was always working overtime.

Now that I had my skinny body swathed in a big T-shirt, I thought I might be in the running with Gretchen, for a change. "How's my hair?" I asked her. I needn't have bothered.

As I swung my hand up to smooth a few

flyaway strands, my bracelet caught in the wire mesh of a trash can. In my surprise, I fell over backward, bringing the trash can — and its contents — over on me. The trash can, which weighed at least a ton, pinned me to the boardwalk like a dead fly. I couldn't move and I was covered with greasy hamburger wrappers, sticky ice cream cones, napkins, drink cups, and a dozen other things I didn't want to identify too closely.

"Kobie! What are you doing down there? Get up! Here he comes!"

"I can't! I'm caught on something."

Gretchen grabbed at the trash can but I still had my bracelet tangled in the mesh and she only succeeded in just about pulling my arm from the socket. "You do this every single time, Kobie. Make a spectacle of yourself in front of a cute boy. I could just die!"

"What about me?" The dregs of a grape soda dribbled down my neck. "Do you think I do these things on purpose?"

"He's almost here! Get up!" Gretchen screamed, letting go of the trash can. I felt a half-eaten candy apple attach itself to my left arm like a leech.

"Just leave me here," I moaned. "Throw your towel over me — maybe he'll think I belong here."

"Honestly, Kobie Roberts. I can't take you any place."

"I know. This is as bad as the time on that field trip when the guide got his badge caught on my sweater at the top of the Washington Monument and tried to drag me backward down all nine hundred and twenty-seven steps."

"Worse," Gretchen said. "Kobie, he's only two feet away. Can't you get up?"

"If I do, I'll be all covered with trash. It's best I just lie here, Gretch." People were staring and pointing at me. I had become the latest boardwalk attraction. See the girl wrestle with the Mangler, the world's only attack trash can.

Managing to unfasten my bracelet at last, I heaved the trash can over and struggled to my feet, trailing bits of debris. I must have looked like a walking advertisement for "Don't Litter America."

"Where is he?" I asked.

"Too late, he's gone. And he was with another girl," Gretchen reported sadly.

"Figures." I sighed, flicking a banana peel off my sleeve. "Do you think next year will be any easier?"

"I don't know."

I didn't, either. But secretly, I was holding out for fourteen. Now *that* will be my year.